Kenneth Kimble
1999

"I put my hand to my hip pocket."

TALES OF THE FISH PATROL

JACK LONDON

WITH ILLUSTRATIONS BY
GEORGE VARIAN

Star Rover House

Contents

Illustrations

I

WHITE AND YELLOW

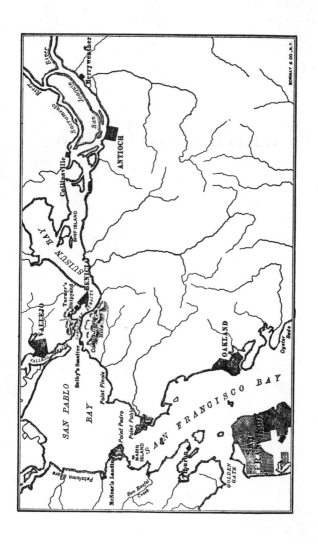

BORMAY & CO., N.Y.

WHITE AND YELLOW

SAN FRANCISCO BAY is so large that often its storms are more disastrous to ocean-going craft than is the ocean itself in its violent moments. The waters of the bay contain all manner of fish, wherefore its surface is ploughed by the keels of all manner of fishing boats manned by all manner of fishermen. To protect the fish from this motley floating population many wise laws have been passed, and there is a fish patrol to see that these laws are enforced. Exciting times are the lot of the fish patrol: in its history more than one dead patrolman has marked defeat, and more often dead fishermen across their illegal nets have marked success.

Wildest among the fisher-folk may be accounted the Chinese shrimp-catchers. It is the habit of the shrimp to crawl along the bottom in vast armies till it reaches fresh water, when it turns about and crawls back again to the salt. And where the tide ebbs and flows, the Chinese sink great bag-nets to the bottom, with gaping mouths, into which the shrimp crawls and from which it is transferred to the boiling-pot. This in itself would not be bad, were it not for the small mesh of the nets, so small that the tiniest fishes, little new-hatched things not a quarter of an inch long, cannot pass through. The beautiful beaches of Points Pedro and Pablo, where are the shrimp-catchers' villages, are made fearful by the stench from myriads of decaying fish, and against this wasteful destruction it has ever been the duty of the fish patrol to act.

When I was a youngster of sixteen, a good sloop-sailor and all-round bay-waterman, my sloop, the *Reindeer*, was chartered by the Fish Commission, and I became for the time being a deputy patrol-man. After a deal of work among the Greek fishermen of the Upper Bay and rivers, where knives flashed at the beginning of trouble and men permitted themselves to be made prisoners only after a revolver was thrust in their faces, we hailed with delight an expedition to the Lower Bay against the Chinese shrimp-catchers.

There were six of us, in two boats, and to avoid suspicion we ran down after dark and dropped anchor under a projecting bluff of land known as Point Pinole. As the east paled with the first light of dawn we got under way again, and hauled close on the land breeze as we slanted across the bay toward Point Pedro. The morning mists curled and clung to the water so that we could see nothing, but we busied ourselves driving the chill from our bodies with hot coffee. Also we had to devote ourselves to the miserable task of bailing, for in some incomprehensible way the *Reindeer* had sprung a generous leak. Half the night had been spent in overhauling the ballast and exploring the seams, but the labor had been without avail. The water still poured in, and perforce we doubled up in the cockpit and tossed it out again.

After coffee, three of the men withdrew to the other boat, a Columbia River salmon boat, leaving three of us in the *Reindeer*. Then the two craft proceeded in company till the sun showed over the eastern sky-line. Its fiery rays dispelled the cling-ing vapors, and there, before our eyes, like a picture, lay the shrimp fleet, spread out in a great half-moon, the tips of the crescent fully three miles apart, and each junk moored fast to the buoy of a shrimp-net. But there was no stir, no sign of life.

The situation dawned upon us. While waiting for slack water, in which to lift their heavy nets from the bed of the bay, the Chinese had all gone to sleep below. We were elated, and our plan of battle was swiftly formed.

"Throw each of your two men on to a junk," whispered Le Grant to me from the salmon boat. "And you make fast to a third yourself. We'll do the same, and there's no reason in the world why we shouldn't capture six junks at the least."

Then we separated. I put the *Rein-deer* about on the other tack, ran up under the lee of a junk, shivered the mainsail into the wind and lost headway, and forged past the stern of the junk so slowly and so near that one of the patrolmen stepped lightly aboard. Then I kept off, filled the mainsail, and bore away for a second junk.

Up to this time there had been no noise, but from the first junk captured by the salmon boat an uproar now broke forth. There was shrill Oriental yelling, a pistol shot, and more yelling.

"It's all up. They're warning the others," said George, the remaining patrolman, as he stood beside me in the cockpit.

By this time we were in the thick of the fleet, and the alarm was spreading with incredible swiftness. The decks were beginning to swarm with half-awakened and half-naked Chinese. Cries and yells of warning and anger were flying over the quiet water, and somewhere a conch shell was being blown with great success. To the right of us I saw the captain of a junk chop away his mooring line with an axe and spring to help his crew at the hoisting of the huge, outlandish lug-sail. But to the left the first heads were popping up from below on another junk, and I rounded up the *Reindeer* alongside long enough for George to spring aboard.

The whole fleet was now under way. In addition to the sails they had gotten out long sweeps, and the bay was being ploughed in every direction by the fleeing junks. I was now alone in the *Reindeer*, seeking feverishly to capture a third prize. The first junk I took after was a clean miss, for it trimmed its sheets and shot away surprisingly into the wind. By fully half a point it outpointed the *Reindeer*, and I began to feel respect for the clumsy craft. Realizing the hopelessness of the pursuit, I filled away, threw out the main-sheet, and drove down before the wind upon the junks to leeward, where I had them at a disadvantage.

The one I had selected wavered indecisively before me, and, as I swung wide to make the boarding gentle, filled suddenly and darted away, the swart Mongols shouting a wild rhythm as they bent to the sweeps. But I had been ready for this. I luffed suddenly. Putting the tiller hard down, and holding it down with my body, I brought the main-sheet in, hand over hand, on the run, so as to retain all possible striking force. The two starboard sweeps of the junk were crumpled up, and then the two boats came together with a crash. The *Reindeer's* bowsprit, like a monstrous hand, reached over and ripped out the junk's chunky mast and towering sail.

This was met by a curdling yell of rage. A big Chinaman, remarkably evil-looking, with his head swathed in a yellow silk handkerchief and face badly pock-marked, planted a pike-pole on the *Reindeer's* bow and began to shove the entangled boats apart. Pausing long enough to let go the jib halyards, and just as the *Reindeer* cleared and began to drift astern, I leaped aboard the junk with a line and made fast. He of the yellow handkerchief and pock-marked face came toward me threateningly, but I put my hand into my hip pocket, and he hesitated. I was unarmed, but the Chinese have learned to be fastidiously careful of American hip pockets, and it was upon this that I depended to keep him and his savage crew at a distance.

I ordered him to drop the anchor at the junk's bow, to which he replied, "No sabbe." The crew responded in like fashion, and though I made my meaning plain by signs, they refused to understand. Realizing the inexpediency of discussing the matter, I went forward myself, overran the line, and let the anchor go.

"Now get aboard, four of you," I said in a loud voice, indicating with my fingers that four of them were to go with me and the fifth was to remain by the junk. The Yellow Handkerchief hesitated; but I repeated the order fiercely (much more fiercely than I felt), at the same time sending my hand to my hip. Again the Yellow Handkerchief was overawed, and with surly

looks he led three of his men aboard the
Reindeer. I cast off at once, and, leaving
the jib down, steered a course for George's
junk. Here it was easier, for there were
two of us, and George had a pistol to fall
back on if it came to the worst. And here,
as with my junk, four Chinese were transferred to the sloop and one left behind to
take care of things.

Four more were added to our passenger
list from the third junk. By this time the
salmon boat had collected its twelve prisoners and came alongside, badly overloaded.
To make matters worse, as it was a small
boat, the patrolmen were so jammed in
with their prisoners that they would have
little chance in case of trouble.

"You'll have to help us out," said Le
Grant.

I looked over my prisoners, who had

crowded into the cabin and on top of it. "I can take three," I answered.

"Make it four," he suggested, "and I'll take Bill with me." (Bill was the third patrolman.) "We haven't elbow room here, and in case of a scuffle one white to every two of them will be just about the right proportion."

The exchange was made, and the salmon boat got up its spritsail and headed down the bay toward the marshes off San Rafael. I ran up the jib and followed with the *Reindeer*. San Rafael, where we were to turn our catch over to the authorities, communicated with the bay by way of a long and tortuous slough, or marshland creek, which could be navigated only when the tide was in. Slack water had come, and, as the ebb was commencing, there was need for hurry if we cared to escape waiting half a day for the next tide.

But the land breeze had begun to die away with the rising sun, and now came only in failing puffs. The salmon boat got out its oars and soon left us far astern. Some of the Chinese stood in the forward part of the cockpit, near the cabin doors, and once, as I leaned over the cockpit rail to flatten down the jib-sheet a bit, I felt some one brush against my hip pocket. I made no sign, but out of the corner of my eye I saw that the Yellow Handkerchief had discovered the emptiness of the pocket which had hitherto overawed him.

To make matters serious, during all the excitement of boarding the junks the *Reindeer* had not been bailed, and the water was beginning to slush over the cockpit floor. The shrimp-catchers pointed at it and looked to me questioningly.

"Yes," I said. "Bime by, allee same

dlown, velly quick, you no bail now. Sabbe?"

No, they did not "sabbe," or at least they shook their heads to that effect, though they chattered most comprehendingly to one another in their own lingo. I pulled up three or four of the bottom boards, got a couple of buckets from a locker, and by unmistakable sign-language invited them to fall to.   But they laughed, and some crowded into the cabin and some climbed up on top.

Their laughter was not good laughter. There was a hint of menace in it, a maliciousness which their black looks verified. The Yellow Handkerchief, since his discovery of my empty pocket, had become most insolent in his bearing, and he wormed about among the other prisoners, talking to them with great earnestness.

Swallowing my chagrin, I stepped down

into the cockpit and began throwing out the water. But hardly had I begun, when the boom swung overhead, the mainsail filled with a jerk, and the *Reindeer* heeled over. The day wind was springing up. George was the veriest of landlubbers, so I was forced to give over bailing and take the tiller. The wind was blowing directly off Point Pedro and the high mountains behind, and because of this was squally and uncertain, half the time bellying the canvas out, and the other half flapping it idly.

George was about the most all-round helpless man I had ever met. Among his other disabilities, he was a consumptive, and I knew that if he attempted to bail, it might bring on a hemorrhage. Yet the rising water warned me that something must be done. Again I ordered the shrimp-catchers to lend a hand with the buckets. They laughed defiantly, and those inside the cabin, the water up to their ankles, shouted back and forth with those on top.

"You'd better get out your gun and make them bail," I said to George.

But he shook his head and showed all too plainly that he was afraid. The Chinese could see the funk he was in as well as I could, and their insolence became insufferable. Those in the cabin broke into the food lockers, and those above scrambled down and joined them in a feast on our crackers and canned goods.

"What do we care?" George said weakly.

I was fuming with helpless anger. "If they get out of hand, it will be too late to care. The best thing you can do is to get them in check right now."

The water was rising higher and higher, and the gusts, forerunners of a steady breeze, were growing stiffer and stiffer. And between the gusts, the prisoners, having gotten away with a week's grub, took to crowding first to one side and then to the other till the *Reindeer* rocked like a cockle-shell. Yellow Handkerchief approached me, and, pointing out his village on the Point Pedro beach, gave me to understand that if I turned the *Reindeer* in that direction and put them ashore, they, in turn, would go to bailing. By now the water in the cabin was up to the bunks, and the bed-clothes were sopping. It was a foot deep on the cockpit floor. Nevertheless I refused, and I could see by George's face that he was disappointed.

"If you don't show some nerve, they'll rush us and throw us overboard," I said to him. "Better give me your revolver, if you want to be safe."

"The safest thing to do," he chattered cravenly, "is to put them ashore.   I, for one, don't want to be drowned for the sake of a handful of dirty Chinamen."

"And I, for another, don't care to give in to a handful of dirty Chinamen to escape drowning," I answered hotly.

"You'll sink the *Reindeer* under us all at this rate," he whined.   "And what good that'll do I can't see."

"Every man to his taste," I retorted.

He made no reply, but I could see he was trembling pitifully. Between the threatening Chinese and the rising water he was beside himself with fright; and, more than the Chinese and the water, I feared him and what his fright might impel him to do. I could see him casting longing glances at the small skiff towing astern, so in the next calm I hauled the skiff alongside. As I did so his eyes brightened with hope; but before he could guess my intention, I stove the frail bottom through with a hand-axe, and the skiff filled to its gunwales.

"It's sink or float together," I said. "And if you'll give me your revolver, I'll have the *Reindeer* bailed out in a jiffy."

"They're too many for us," he whimpered. "We can't fight them all."

I turned my back on him in disgust. The salmon boat had long since passed from sight behind a little archipelago known as the Marin Islands, so no help could be looked for from that quarter. Yellow Handkerchief came up to me in a familiar manner, the water in the cockpit slushing against his legs. I did not like his looks. I felt that beneath the pleasant smile he was trying to put on his face there was an ill purpose. I ordered him back, and so sharply that he obeyed.

"Now keep your distance," I commanded, "and don't you come closer!"

"Wha' fo'?" he demanded indignantly. "I t'ink-um talkee talkee heap good."

"Talkee talkee," I answered bitterly, for I knew now that he had understood all that passed between George and me. "What for talkee talkee? You no sabbe talkee talkee."

He grinned in a sickly fashion. "Yep, I sabbe velly much. I honest Chinaman."

"All right," I answered. "You sabbe talkee talkee, then you bail water plenty plenty. After that we talkee talkee."

He shook his head, at the same time pointing over his shoulder to his comrades. "No can do. Velly bad Chinamen, heap velly bad. I t'ink-um —"

"Stand back!" I shouted, for I had noticed his hand disappear beneath his blouse and his body prepare for a spring.

Disconcerted, he went back into the cabin, to hold a council, apparently, from the way the jabbering broke forth. The *Reindeer* was very deep in the water, and her movements had grown quite loggy. In a rough sea she would have inevitably swamped; but the wind, when it did blow, was off the land, and scarcely a ripple disturbed the surface of the bay.

"I think you'd better head for the beach," George said abruptly, in a manner that told me his fear had forced him to make up his mind to some course of action.

"I think not," I answered shortly.

"I command you," he said in a bullying tone.

"I was commanded to bring these prisoners into San Rafael," was my reply.

Our voices were raised, and the sound of the altercation brought the Chinese out of the cabin.

"Now will you head for the beach?"

This from George, and I found myself looking into the muzzle of his revolver — of the revolver he dared to use on me, but was too cowardly to use on the prisoners.

My brain seemed smitten with a dazzling brightness. The whole situation, in all its bearings, was focussed sharply before me — the shame of losing the prisoners, the worthlessness and cowardice of George, the meeting with Le Grant and the other patrolmen and the lame explanation; and then there was the fight I had fought so hard, victory wrenched from me just as I thought I had it within my grasp. And out of the tail of my eye I could see the Chinese crowding together by the cabin doors and leering triumphantly. It would never do.

I threw my hand up and my head down. The first act elevated the muzzle, and the second removed my head from the path of the bullet which went whistling past. One hand closed on George's wrist, the other on the revolver. Yellow Handkerchief and his gang sprang toward me. It was now or never. Putting all my strength into a sudden effort, I swung George's body forward to meet them. Then I pulled back with equal suddenness, ripping the revolver out of his fingers and jerking him off his feet. He fell against Yellow Handkerchief's knees, who stumbled over him, and the pair wallowed in the bailing hole where the cockpit floor was torn open. The next instant I was covering them with my revolver, and the wild shrimp-catchers were cowering and cringing away.

But I swiftly discovered that there was all the difference in the world between shooting men who are attacking and men who are doing nothing more than simply refusing to obey. For obey they would not when I ordered them into the bailing hole. I threatened them with the revolver, but they sat stolidly in the flooded cabin and on the roof and would not move.

Fifteen minutes passed, the *Reindeer* sinking deeper and deeper, her mainsail flapping in the calm. But from off the Point Pedro shore I saw a dark line form on the water and travel toward us. It was the steady breeze I had been expecting so long. I called to the Chinese and pointed it out. They hailed it with exclamations. Then I pointed to the sail and to the water in the *Reindeer*, and indicated by signs that when the wind reached the sail, what of the water aboard we would capsize. But they jeered defiantly, for they knew it was in my power to luff the helm and let go the main-sheet, so as to spill the wind and escape damage.

But my mind was made up. I hauled in the main-sheet a foot or two, took a turn with it, and bracing my feet, put my back against the tiller. This left me one hand for the sheet and one for the revolver. The dark line drew nearer, and I could see them looking from me to it and back again with an apprehension they could not successfully conceal. My brain and will and endurance were pitted against theirs, and the problem was which could stand the strain of imminent death the longer and not give in.

Then the wind struck us. The main-sheet tautened with a brisk rattling of the blocks, the boom uplifted, the sail bellied out, and the *Reindeer* heeled over — over, and over, till the lee-rail went under, the deck went under, the cabin windows went under, and the bay began to pour in over the cockpit rail. So violently had she heeled over, that the men in the cabin had been thrown on top of one another into the lee bunk, where they squirmed and twisted and were washed about, those underneath being perilously near to drowning.

The wind freshened a bit, and the *Reindeer* went over farther than ever. For the moment I thought she was gone, and I knew that another puff like that and she surely would go. While I pressed her under and debated whether I should give up or not, the Chinese cried for mercy. I think it was the sweetest sound I have ever heard.

And then, and not until then, did I luff up and ease out the main-sheet. The *Reindeer* righted very slowly, and when she was on an even keel was so much awash that I doubted if she could be saved.

But the Chinese scrambled madly into the cockpit and fell to bailing with buckets, pots, pans, and everything they could lay hands on. It was a beautiful sight to see that water flying over the side! And when the *Reindeer* was high and proud on the water once more, we dashed away with the breeze on our quarter, and at the last possible moment crossed the mud flats and entered the slough.

The spirit of the Chinese was broken, and so docile did they become that ere we made San Rafael they were out with the tow-rope, Yellow Handkerchief at the head of the line. As for George, it was his last trip with the fish patrol. He did not care for that sort of thing, he explained, and he thought a clerkship ashore was good enough for him. And we thought so, too.

II

THE KING OF THE GREEKS

THE KING OF THE GREEKS

BIG ALEC had never been captured by the fish patrol. It was his boast that no man could take him alive, and it was his history that of the many men who had tried to take him dead none had succeeded. It was also history that at least two patrolmen who had tried to take him dead had died themselves. Further, no man violated the fish laws more systematically and deliberately than Big Alec.

He was called "Big Alec" because of his gigantic stature. His height was six feet three inches, and he was correspondingly broad-shouldered and deep-chested. He was splendidly muscled and hard as steel, and there were innumerable stories in circulation among the fisher-folk concerning his prodigious strength. He was as bold and dominant of spirit as he was strong of body, and because of this he was widely known by another name, that of "The King of the Greeks." The fishing population was largely composed of Greeks, and they looked up to him and obeyed him as their chief. And as their chief, he fought their fights for them, saw that they were protected, saved them from the law when they fell into its clutches, and made them stand by one another and himself in time of trouble.

In the old days, the fish patrol had attempted his capture many disastrous times and had finally given it over, so that when the word was out that he was coming to Benicia, I was most anxious to see him.

But I did not have to hunt him up. In his usual bold way, the first thing he did on arriving was to hunt us up. Charley Le Grant and I at the time were under a patrolman named Carmintel, and the three of us were on the *Reindeer*, preparing for a trip, when Big Alec stepped aboard. Carmintel evidently knew him, for they shook hands in recognition. Big Alec took no notice of Charley or me.

"I've come down to fish sturgeon a couple of months," he said to Carmintel.

His eyes flashed with challenge as he spoke, and we noticed the patrolman's eyes drop before him.

"That's all right, Alec," Carmintel said in a low voice. "I'll not bother you. Come on into the cabin, and we'll talk things over," he added.

When they had gone inside and shut the

doors after them, Charley winked with slow deliberation at me. But I was only a youngster, and new to men and the ways of some men, so I did not understand. Nor did Charley explain, though I felt there was something wrong about the business.

Leaving them to their conference, at Charley's suggestion we boarded our skiff and pulled over to the Old Steamboat Wharf, where Big Alec's ark was lying. An ark is a house-boat of small though comfortable dimensions, and is as necessary to the Upper Bay fisherman as are nets and boats. We were both curious to see Big Alec's ark, for history said that it had been the scene of more than one pitched battle, and that it was riddled with bullet-holes.

We found the holes (stopped with wooden plugs and painted over), but there were not so many as I had expected. Charley noted my look of disappointment, and laughed; and then to comfort me he gave an authentic account of one expedition which had descended upon Big Alec's floating home to capture him, alive preferably, dead if necessary. At the end of half a day's fighting, the patrolmen had drawn off in wrecked boats, with one of their number killed and three wounded. And when they returned next morning with reënforcements they found only the mooring-stakes of Big Alec's ark; the ark itself remained hidden for months in the fastnesses of the Suisun tules.

"But why was he not hanged for murder?" I demanded. "Surely the United States is powerful enough to bring such a man to justice."

"He gave himself up and stood trial,"

Charley answered. "It cost him fifty thousand dollars to win the case, which he did on technicalities and with the aid of the best lawyers in the state. Every Greek fisherman on the river contributed to the sum. Big Alec levied and collected the tax, for all the world like a king. The United States may be all-powerful, my lad, but the fact remains that Big Alec is a king inside the United States, with a country and subjects all his own."

"But what are you going to do about his fishing for sturgeon? He's bound to fish with a 'Chinese line.'"

Charley shrugged his shoulders. "We'll see what we will see," he said enigmatically.

Now a "Chinese line" is a cunning device invented by the people whose name it bears. By a simple system of floats, weights, and anchors, thousands of hooks, each on a separate leader, are suspended at a distance of from six inches to a foot above the bottom. The remarkable thing about such a line is the hook. It is barbless, and in place of the barb, the hook is filed long and tapering to a point as sharp as that of a needle. These hooks are only a few inches apart, and when several thousand of them are suspended just above the bottom, like a fringe, for a couple of hundred fathoms, they present a formidable obstacle to the fish that travel along the bottom.

Such a fish is the sturgeon, which goes rooting along like a pig, and indeed is often called "pig-fish." Pricked by the first hook it touches, the sturgeon gives a startled leap and comes into contact with half a dozen more hooks. Then it threshes about wildly, until it receives hook after hook in its soft flesh; and the hooks, straining from many different angles, hold the luckless fish fast until it is drowned. Because no sturgeon can pass through a Chinese line, the device is called a trap in the fish laws; and because it bids fair to exterminate the sturgeon, it is branded by the fish laws as illegal. And such a line, we were confident, Big Alec intended setting, in open and flagrant violation of the law.

Several days passed after the visit of Big Alec, during which Charley and I kept a sharp watch on him. He towed his ark around the Solano Wharf and into the big bight at Turner's Shipyard. The bight we knew to be good ground for sturgeon, and there we felt sure the King of the Greeks intended to begin operations. The tide circled like a mill-race in and out of this bight, and made it possible to raise, lower, or set a Chinese line only at slack water. So between the tides Charley and I made it a point for one or the other of us to keep a lookout from the Solano Wharf.

On the fourth day I was lying in the sun behind the stringer-piece of the wharf, when I saw a skiff leave the distant shore and pull out into the bight. In an instant the glasses were at my eyes and I was following every movement of the skiff. There were two men in it, and though it was a good mile away, I made out one of them to be Big Alec; and ere the skiff returned to shore I made out enough more to know that the Greek had set his line.

"Big Alec has a Chinese line out in the bight off Turner's Shipyard," Charley Le Grant said that afternoon to Carmintel.

A fleeting expression of annoyance passed over the patrolman's face, and then he said, "Yes?" in an absent way, and that was all.

Charley bit his lip with suppressed anger and turned on his heel.

"Are you game, my lad?" he said to me later on in the evening, just as we finished washing down the *Reindeer's* decks and were preparing to turn in.

A lump came up in my throat, and I could only nod my head.

"Well, then," and Charley's eyes glittered in a determined way, "we've got to capture Big Alec between us, you and I, and we've got to do it in spite of Carmintel. Will you lend a hand?"

"It's a hard proposition, but we can do it," he added after a pause.

"Of course we can," I supplemented enthusiastically.

And then he said, "Of course we can,"

and we shook hands on it and went to bed.

But it was no easy task we had set ourselves. In order to convict a man of illegal fishing, it was necessary to catch him in the act with all the evidence of the crime about him — the hooks, the lines, the fish, and the man himself. This meant that we must take Big Alec on the open water, where he could see us coming and prepare for us one of the warm receptions for which he was noted.

"There's no getting around it," Charley said one morning. "If we can only get alongside it's an even toss, and there's nothing left for us but to try and get alongside. Come on, lad."

We were in the Columbia River salmon boat, the one we had used against the Chinese shrimp-catchers. Slack water had come, and as we dropped around the end of the Solano Wharf we saw Big Alec at work, running his line and removing the fish.

"Change places," Charley commanded, "and steer just astern of him as though you're going into the shipyard."

I took the tiller, and Charley sat down on a thwart amidships, placing his revolver handily beside him.

"If he begins to shoot," he cautioned, "get down in the bottom and steer from there, so that nothing more than your hand will be exposed."

I nodded, and we kept silent after that, the boat slipping gently through the water and Big Alec growing nearer and nearer. We could see him quite plainly, gaffing the sturgeon and throwing them into the boat while his companion ran the line and cleared the hooks as he dropped them back into the water. Nevertheless, we were five hundred yards away when the big fisherman hailed us.

"Here! You! What do you want?" he shouted.

"Keep going," Charley whispered, "just as though you didn't hear him."

The next few moments were very anxious ones. The fisherman was studying us sharply, while we were gliding up on him every second.

"You keep off if you know what's good for you!" he called out suddenly, as though he had made up his mind as to who and what we were. "If you don't, I'll fix you!"

He brought a rifle to his shoulder and trained it on me.

"Now will you keep off?" he demanded.

I could hear Charley groan with disappointment. "Keep off," he whispered; "it's all up for this time."

I put up the tiller and eased the sheet, and the salmon boat ran off five or six points. Big Alec watched us till we were out of range, when he returned to his work.

"You'd better leave Big Alec alone," Carmintel said, rather sourly, to Charley that night.

"So he's been complaining to you, has he?" Charley said significantly.

Carmintel flushed painfully. "You'd better leave him alone, I tell you," he repeated. "He's a dangerous man, and it won't pay to fool with him."

"Yes," Charley answered softly; "I've heard that it pays better to leave him alone."

This was a direct thrust at Carmintel, and we could see by the expression of his face that it sank home. For it was common knowledge that Big Alec was as willing to bribe as to fight, and that of late years more than one patrolman had handled the fisherman's money.

"Do you mean to say —" Carmintel began, in a bullying tone.

But Charley cut him off shortly. "I mean to say nothing," he said. "You heard what I said, and if the cap fits, why —"

He shrugged his shoulders, and Carmintel glowered at him, speechless.

"What we want is imagination," Charley said to me one day, when we had attempted to creep upon Big Alec in the gray of dawn and had been shot at for our trouble.

And thereafter, and for many days, I cudgelled my brains trying to imagine some possible way by which two men, on an open stretch of water, could capture another who knew how to use a rifle and was never to be found without one. Regularly, every slack water, without slyness, boldly and openly in the broad day, Big Alec was to be seen running his line. And what made it particularly exasperating was the fact that every fisherman, from Benicia to Vallejo, knew that he was successfully defying us. Carmintel also bothered us, for he kept us busy among the shad-fishers of San Pablo, so that we had little time to spare on the King of the Greeks. But Charley's wife and children lived at Benicia, and we had made the place our headquarters, so that we always returned to it.

"I'll tell you what we can do," I said, after several fruitless weeks had passed; "we can wait some slack water till Big Alec has run his line and gone ashore with the fish, and then we can go out and capture the line. It will put him to time and expense to make another, and then we'll figure to capture that too. If we can't capture him, we can discourage him, you see."

Charley saw, and said it wasn't a bad idea. We watched our chance, and the next low-water slack, after Big Alec had removed the fish from the line and returned ashore, we went out in the salmon boat. We had the bearings of the line from shore marks, and we knew we would have no difficulty in locating it. The first of the flood tide was setting in, when we ran below where we thought the line was stretched and dropped over a fishing-boat anchor. Keeping a short rope to the anchor, so that it barely touched the bottom, we dragged it slowly along until it stuck and the boat fetched up hard and fast.

"We've got it," Charley cried. "Come on and lend a hand to get it in."

Together we hove up the rope till the anchor came in sight with the sturgeon line caught across one of the flukes. Scores of the murderous-looking hooks flashed into sight as we cleared the anchor, and we had just started to run along the line to the end where we could begin to lift it, when a sharp thud in the boat startled us. We looked about, but saw nothing and returned to our work. An instant later there was a similar sharp thud and the gunwale splintered between Charley's body and mine.

"That's remarkably like a bullet, lad," he said reflectively. "And it's a long shot Big Alec's making."

"And he's using smokeless powder," he concluded, after an examination of the mile-distant shore. "That's why we can't hear the report."

I looked at the shore, but could see no

sign of Big Alec, who was undoubtedly hidden in some rocky nook with us at his mercy. A third bullet struck the water, glanced, passed singing over our heads, and struck the water again beyond.

"I guess we'd better get out of this," Charley remarked coolly. "What do you think, lad?"

I thought so, too, and said we didn't want the line anyway. Whereupon we cast off and hoisted the spritsail. The bullets ceased at once, and we sailed away, unpleasantly confident that Big Alec was laughing at our discomfiture.

And more than that, the next day on the fishing wharf, where we were inspecting nets, he saw fit to laugh and sneer at us, and this before all the fishermen. Charley's face went black with anger; but beyond promising Big Alec that in the end he would surely land him behind the bars, he controlled himself and said nothing. The King of the Greeks made his boast that no fish patrol had ever taken him or ever could take him, and the fishermen cheered him and said it was true. They grew excited, and it looked like trouble for a while; but Big Alec asserted his kingship and quelled them.

Carmintel also laughed at Charley, and dropped sarcastic remarks, and made it hard for him. But Charley refused to be angered, though he told me in confidence that he intended to capture Big Alec if it took all the rest of his life to accomplish it.

"I don't know how I'll do it," he said, "but do it I will, as sure as I am Charley Le Grant. The idea will come to me at the right and proper time, never fear."

And at the right time it came, and most

"He saw fit to laugh and sneer at us, before all the fishermen."

unexpectedly. Fully a month had passed, and we were constantly up and down the river, and down and up the bay, with no spare moments to devote to the particular fisherman who ran a Chinese line in the bight of Turner's Shipyard. We had called in at Selby's Smelter one afternoon, while on patrol work, when all unknown to us our opportunity happened along. It appeared in the guise of a helpless yacht loaded with seasick people, so we could hardly be expected to recognize it as the opportunity. It was a large sloop-yacht, and it was helpless inasmuch as the trade-wind was blowing half a gale and there were no capable sailors aboard.

From the wharf at Selby's we watched with careless interest the lubberly manœuvre performed of bringing the yacht to anchor, and the equally lubberly manœuvre

of sending the small boat ashore. A very
miserable-looking man in draggled ducks,
after nearly swamping the boat in the heavy
seas, passed us the painter and climbed
out. He staggered about as though the
wharf were rolling, and told us his troubles,
which were the troubles of the yacht. The
only rough-weather sailor aboard, the man
on whom they all depended, had been called
back to San Francisco by a telegram, and
they had attempted to continue the cruise
alone. The high wind and big seas of San
Pablo Bay had been too much for them;
all hands were sick, nobody knew anything or could do anything; and so they
had run in to the smelter either to desert
the yacht or to get somebody to bring it
to Benicia. In short, did we know of
any sailors who would bring the yacht into
Benicia ?

Charley looked at me. The *Reindeer* was lying in a snug place. We had nothing on hand in the way of patrol work till midnight. With the wind then blowing, we could sail the yacht into Benicia in a couple of hours, have several more hours ashore, and come back to the smelter on the evening train.

"All right, captain," Charley said to the disconsolate yachtsman, who smiled in sickly fashion at the title.

"I'm only the owner," he explained.

We rowed him aboard in much better style than he had come ashore, and saw for ourselves the helplessness of the passengers. There were a dozen men and women, and all of them too sick even to appear grateful at our coming. The yacht was rolling savagely, broad on, and no sooner had the owner's feet touched the deck than he collapsed and joined the others. Not one was able to bear a hand, so Charley and I between us cleared the badly tangled running gear, got up sail, and hoisted anchor.

It was a rough trip, though a swift one. The Carquinez Straits were a welter of foam and smother, and we came through them wildly before the wind, the big mainsail alternately dipping and flinging its boom skyward as we tore along. But the people did not mind. They did not mind anything. Two or three, including the owner, sprawled in the cockpit, shuddering when the yacht lifted and raced and sank dizzily into the trough, and betweenwhiles regarding the shore with yearning eyes. The rest were huddled on the cabin floor among the cushions. Now and again some one groaned, but for the most part they were as limp as so many dead persons.

As the bight at Turner's Shipyard opened out, Charley edged into it to get the smoother water. Benicia was in view, and we were bowling along over comparatively easy water, when a speck of a boat danced up ahead of us, directly in our course. It was low-water slack. Charley and I looked at each other. No word was spoken, but at once the yacht began a most astonishing performance, veering and yawing as though the greenest of amateurs was at the wheel. It was a sight for sailormen to see. To all appearances, a runaway yacht was careering madly over the bight, and now and again yielding a little bit to control in a desperate effort to make Benicia.

The owner forgot his seasickness long enough to look anxious. The speck of a boat grew larger and larger, till we could see Big Alec and his partner, with a turn of the sturgeon line around a cleat, resting from their labor to laugh at us. Charley pulled his sou'wester over his eyes, and I followed his example, though I could not guess the idea he evidently had in mind and intended to carry into execution.

We came foaming down abreast of the skiff, so close that we could hear above the wind the voices of Big Alec and his mate as they shouted at us with all the scorn that professional watermen feel for amateurs, especially when amateurs are making fools of themselves.

We thundered on past the fishermen, and nothing had happened. Charley grinned at the disappointment he saw in my face, and then shouted:

"Stand by the main-sheet to jibe!"

He put the wheel hard over, and the yacht whirled around obediently. The main-sheet slacked and dipped, then shot over our heads after the boom and tautened with a crash on the traveller. The yacht heeled over almost on her beam ends, and a great wail went up from the seasick passengers as they swept across the cabin floor in a tangled mass and piled into a heap in the starboard bunks.

But we had no time for them. The yacht, completing the manœuvre, headed into the wind with slatting canvas, and righted to an even keel. We were still plunging ahead, and directly in our path was the skiff. I saw Big Alec dive overboard and his mate leap for our bowsprit. Then came the crash as we struck the boat, and a series of grinding bumps as it passed under our bottom.

"That fixes his rifle," I heard Charley mutter, as he sprang upon the deck to look for Big Alec somewhere astern.

The wind and sea quickly stopped our forward movement, and we began to drift backward over the spot where the skiff had been. Big Alec's black head and swarthy face popped up within arm's reach; and all unsuspecting and very angry with what he took to be the clumsiness of amateur sailors, he was hauled aboard. Also he was out of breath, for he had dived deep and stayed down long to escape our keel.

The next instant, to the perplexity and consternation of the owner, Charley was on top of Big Alec in the cockpit, and I was helping bind him with gaskets. The owner was dancing excitedly about and demanding an explanation, but by that time Big Alec's partner had crawled aft from the bowsprit and was peering apprehensively over the rail into the cockpit. Charley's arm shot around his neck and the man landed on his back beside Big Alec.

"More gaskets!" Charley shouted, and I made haste to supply them.

The wrecked skiff was rolling sluggishly a short distance to windward, and I trimmed the sheets while Charley took the wheel and steered for it.

"These two men are old offenders," he explained to the angry owner; "and they are most persistent violators of the fish and game laws. You have seen them caught in the act, and you may expect to be subpœnaed as witness for the state when the trial comes off."

As he spoke he rounded alongside the skiff. It had been torn from the line, a section of which was dragging to it. He hauled in forty or fifty feet with a young sturgeon still fast in a tangle of barbless hooks, slashed that much of the line free with his knife, and tossed it into the cockpit beside the prisoners.

"And there's the evidence, Exhibit A, for the people," Charley continued. "Look it over carefully so that you may identify it in the court-room with the time and place of capture."

And then, in triumph, with no more veering and yawing, we sailed into Benicia, the King of the Greeks bound hard and fast in the cockpit, and for the first time in his life a prisoner of the fish patrol.

III

A RAID ON THE OYSTER
PIRATES

A RAID ON THE OYSTER
PIRATES

O F the fish patrolmen under whom
we served at various times, Charley
Le Grant and I were agreed, I
think, that Neil Partington was the best.
He was neither dishonest nor cowardly; and
while he demanded strict obedience when we
were under his orders, at the same time our
relations were those of easy comradeship,
and he permitted us a freedom to which we
were ordinarily unaccustomed, as the present
story will show.

Neil's family lived in Oakland, which is
on the Lower Bay, not more than six miles
across the water from San Francisco. One
day, while scouting among the Chinese
shrimp-catchers of Point Pedro, he received

word that his wife was very ill; and within the hour the *Reindeer* was bowling along for Oakland, with a stiff northwest breeze astern. We ran up the Oakland Estuary and came to anchor, and in the days that followed, while Neil was ashore, we tightened up the *Reindeer's* rigging, overhauled the ballast, scraped down, and put the sloop into thorough shape.

This done, time hung heavy on our hands. Neil's wife was dangerously ill, and the outlook was a week's lie-over, awaiting the crisis. Charley and I roamed the docks, wondering what we should do, and so came upon the oyster fleet lying at the Oakland City Wharf. In the main they were trim, natty boats, made for speed and bad weather, and we sat down on the stringer-piece of the dock to study them.

"A good catch, I guess," Charley said,

pointing to the heaps of oysters, assorted in three sizes, which lay upon their decks.

Pedlers were backing their wagons to the edge of the wharf, and from the bargaining and chaffering that went on, I managed to learn the selling price of the oysters.

"That boat must have at least two hundred dollars' worth aboard," I calculated. "I wonder how long it took to get the load?"

"Three or four days," Charley answered. "Not bad wages for two men — twenty-five dollars a day apiece."

The boat we were discussing, the *Ghost*, lay directly beneath us. Two men composed its crew. One was a squat, broad-shouldered fellow with remarkably long and gorilla-like arms, while the other was tall and well proportioned, with clear blue eyes

and a mat of straight black hair. So un-
usual and striking was this combination of
hair and eyes that Charley and I remained
somewhat longer than we intended.

And it was well that we did. A stout,
elderly man, with the dress and carriage of
a successful merchant, came up and stood
beside us, looking down upon the deck of
the *Ghost*. He appeared angry, and the
longer he looked the angrier he grew.

"Those are my oysters," he said at last.
"I know they are my oysters. You raided
my beds last night and robbed me of them."

The tall man and the short man on the
Ghost looked up.

"Hello, Taft," the short man said, with
insolent familiarity. (Among the bayfarers
he had gained the nickname of "The Centipede" on account of his long arms.)
"Hello, Taft," he repeated, with the same

touch of insolence. "Wot 'r you growlin' about now?"

"Those are my oysters — that's what I said. You've stolen them from my beds."

"Yer mighty wise, ain't ye?" was the Centipede's sneering reply. "S'pose you can tell your oysters wherever you see 'em?"

"Now, in my experience," broke in the tall man, "oysters is oysters wherever you find 'em, an' they're pretty much alike all the Bay over, and the world over, too, for that matter. We're not wantin' to quarrel with you, Mr. Taft, but we jes' wish you wouldn't insinuate that them oysters is yours an' that we're thieves an' robbers till you can prove the goods."

"I know they're mine; I'd stake my life on it!" Mr. Taft snorted.

"Prove it," challenged the tall man, who we afterward learned was known as

"The Porpoise" because of his wonderful swimming abilities.

Mr. Taft shrugged his shoulders helplessly. Of course he could not prove the oysters to be his, no matter how certain he might be.

"I'd give a thousand dollars to have you men behind the bars!" he cried. "I'll give fifty dollars a head for your arrest and conviction, all of you!"

A roar of laughter went up from the different boats, for the rest of the pirates had been listening to the discussion.

"There's more money in oysters," the Porpoise remarked dryly.

Mr. Taft turned impatiently on his heel and walked away. From out of the corner of his eye, Charley noted the way he went. Several minutes later, when he had disappeared around a corner, Charley rose lazily to his feet. I followed him, and we sauntered off in the opposite direction to that taken by Mr. Taft.

"Come on! Lively!" Charley whispered, when we passed from the view of the oyster fleet.

Our course was changed at once, and we dodged around corners and raced up and down side-streets till Mr. Taft's generous form loomed up ahead of us.

"I'm going to interview him about that reward," Charley explained, as we rapidly overhauled the oyster-bed owner. "Neil will be delayed here for a week, and you and I might as well be doing something in the meantime. What do you say?"

"Of course, of course," Mr. Taft said, when Charley had introduced himself and explained his errand. "Those thieves are robbing me of thousands of dollars every year, and I shall be glad to break them up at any price, — yes, sir, at any price. As I said, I'll give fifty dollars a head, and call it cheap at that. They've robbed my beds, torn down my signs, terrorized my watchmen, and last year killed one of them. Couldn't prove it. All done in the blackness of night. All I had was a dead watchman and no evidence. The detectives could do nothing. Nobody has been able to do anything with those men. We have never succeeded in arresting one of them. So I say, Mr. — What did you say your name was?"

"Le Grant," Charley answered.

"So I say, Mr. Le Grant, I am deeply obliged to you for the assistance you offer. And I shall be glad, most glad, sir, to co-operate with you in every way. My watchmen and boats are at your disposal. Come

and see me at the San Francisco offices
any time, or telephone at my expense. And
don't be afraid of spending money. I'll
foot your expenses, whatever they are, so
long as they are within reason. The situation is growing desperate, and something
must be done to determine whether I or
that band of ruffians own those oyster
beds."

"Now we'll see Neil," Charley said,
when he had seen Mr. Taft upon his train
to San Francisco.

Not only did Neil Partington interpose
no obstacle to our adventure, but he proved
to be of the greatest assistance. Charley
and I knew nothing of the oyster industry,
while his head was an encyclopædia of
facts concerning it. Also, within an hour
or so, he was able to bring to us a Greek
boy of seventeen or eighteen who knew

thoroughly well the ins and outs of oyster piracy.

At this point I may as well explain that we of the fish patrol were free lances in a way. While Neil Partington, who was a patrolman proper, received a regular salary, Charley and I, being merely deputies, received only what we earned — that is to say, a certain percentage of the fines imposed on convicted violators of the fish laws. Also, any rewards that chanced our way were ours. We offered to share with Partington whatever we should get from Mr. Taft, but the patrolman would not hear of it. He was only too happy, he said, to do a good turn for us, who had done so many for him.

We held a long council of war, and mapped out the following line of action. Our faces were unfamiliar on the Lower

Bay, but as the *Reindeer* was well known as a fish-patrol sloop, the Greek boy, whose name was Nicholas, and I were to sail some innocent-looking craft down to Asparagus Island and join the oyster pirates' fleet. Here, according to Nicholas's description of the beds and the manner of raiding, it was possible for us to catch the pirates in the act of stealing oysters, and at the same time to get them in our power. Charley was to be on the shore, with Mr. Taft's watchmen and a posse of constables, to help us at the right time.

"I know just the boat," Neil said, at the conclusion of the discussion, "a crazy old sloop that's lying over at Tiburon. You and Nicholas can go over by the ferry, charter it for a song, and sail direct for the beds."

"Good luck be with you, boys," he said

at parting, two days later. "Remember, they are dangerous men, so be careful."

Nicholas and I succeeded in chartering the sloop very cheaply; and between laughs, while getting up sail, we agreed that she was even crazier and older than she had been described. She was a big, flat-bottomed, square-sterned craft, sloop-rigged, with a sprung mast, slack rigging, dilapidated sails, and rotten running-gear, clumsy to handle and uncertain in bringing about, and she smelled vilely of coal tar, with which strange stuff she had been smeared from stem to stern and from cabin-roof to centreboard. And to cap it all, *Coal Tar Maggie* was printed in great white letters the whole length of either side.

It was an uneventful though laughable run from Tiburon to Asparagus Island, where we arrived in the afternoon of the

following day. The oyster pirates, a fleet
of a dozen sloops, were lying at anchor on
what was known as the "Deserted Beds."
The *Coal Tar Maggie* came sloshing into
their midst with a light breeze astern, and
they crowded on deck to see us. Nicholas
and I had caught the spirit of the crazy
craft, and we handled her in most lubberly
fashion.

"Wot is it?" some one called.

"Name it 'n' ye kin have it!" called
another.

"I swan naow, ef it ain't the old Ark
itself!" mimicked the Centipede from the
deck of the *Ghost*.

"Hey! Ahoy there, clipper ship!" another wag shouted. "Wot's yer port?"

We took no notice of the joking, but
acted, after the manner of greenhorns, as
though the *Coal Tar Maggie* required our

undivided attention. I rounded her well to windward of the *Ghost*, and Nicholas ran for'ard to drop the anchor. To all appearances it was a bungle, the way the chain tangled and kept the anchor from reaching the bottom. And to all appearances Nicholas and I were terribly excited as we strove to clear it. At any rate, we quite deceived the pirates, who took huge delight in our predicament.

But the chain remained tangled, and amid all kinds of mocking advice we drifted down upon and fouled the *Ghost*, whose bowsprit poked square through our mainsail and ripped a hole in it as big as a barn door. The Centipede and the Porpoise doubled up on the cabin in paroxysms of laughter, and left us to get clear as best we could. This, with much unseamanlike performance, we succeeded in doing, and like-

"The Centipede and the Porpoise doubled up on the cabin
in paroxysms of laughter."

wise in clearing the anchor-chain, of which we let out about three hundred feet. With only ten feet of water under us, this would permit the *Coal Tar Maggie* to swing in a circle six hundred feet in diameter, in which circle she would be able to foul at least half the fleet.

The oyster pirates lay snugly together at short hawsers, the weather being fine, and they protested loudly at our ignorance in putting out such an unwarranted length of anchor-chain. And not only did they protest, for they made us heave it in again, all but thirty feet.

Having sufficiently impressed them with our general lubberliness, Nicholas and I went below to congratulate ourselves and to cook supper. Hardly had we finished the meal and washed the dishes, when a skiff ground against the *Coal Tar Maggie's* side, and heavy feet trampled on deck. Then the Centipede's brutal face appeared in the companionway, and he descended into the cabin, followed by the Porpoise. Before they could seat themselves on a bunk, another skiff came alongside, and another, and another, till the whole fleet was represented by the gathering in the cabin.

"Where'd you swipe the old tub?" asked a squat and hairy man, with cruel eyes and Mexican features.

"Didn't swipe it," Nicholas answered, meeting them on their own ground and encouraging the idea that we had stolen the *Coal Tar Maggie*. "And if we did, what of it?"

"Well, I don't admire your taste, that's all," sneered he of the Mexican features. "I'd rot on the beach first before I'd take a tub that couldn't get out of its own way."

"How were we to know till we tried her?" Nicholas asked, so innocently as to cause a laugh. "And how do you get the oysters?" he hurried on. "We want a load of them; that's what we came for, a load of oysters."

"What d'ye want 'em for?" demanded the Porpoise.

"Oh, to give away to our friends, of course," Nicholas retorted. "That's what you do with yours, I suppose."

This started another laugh, and as our visitors grew more genial we could see that they had not the slightest suspicion of our identity or purpose.

"Didn't I see you on the dock in Oakland the other day?" the Centipede asked suddenly of me.

"Yep," I answered boldly, taking the bull by the horns. "I was watching you fellows and figuring out whether we'd go

oystering or not. It's a pretty good business, I calculate, and so we're going in for
it. That is," I hastened to add, "if you
fellows don't mind."

"I'll tell you one thing, which ain't two
things," he replied, "and that is you'll
have to hump yerself an' get a better boat.
We won't stand to be disgraced by any such
box as this. Understand?"

"Sure," I said. "Soon as we sell some
oysters we'll outfit in style."

"And if you show yerself square an' the
right sort," he went on, "why, you kin
run with us. But if you don't" (here his
voice became stern and menacing), "why,
it'll be the sickest day of yer life. Understand?"

"Sure," I said.

After that and more warning and advice
of similar nature, the conversation became

general, and we learned that the beds were to be raided that very night. As they got into their boats, after an hour's stay, we were invited to join them in the raid with the assurance of "the more the merrier."

"Did you notice that short, Mexican-looking chap?" Nicholas asked, when they had departed to their various sloops. "He's Barchi, of the Sporting Life Gang, and the fellow that came with him is Skilling. They're both out now on five thousand dollars' bail."

I had heard of the Sporting Life Gang before, a crowd of hoodlums and criminals that terrorized the lower quarters of Oakland, and two-thirds of which were usually to be found in state's prison for crimes that ranged from perjury and ballot-box stuffing to murder.

"They are not regular oyster pirates,"

Nicholas continued. "They've just come down for the lark and to make a few dollars. But we'll have to watch out for them."

We sat in the cockpit and discussed the details of our plan till eleven o'clock had passed, when we heard the rattle of an oar in a boat from the direction of the *Ghost*. We hauled up our own skiff, tossed in a few sacks, and rowed over. There we found all the skiffs assembling, it being the intention to raid the beds in a body.

To my surprise, I found barely a foot of water where we had dropped anchor in ten feet. It was the big June run-out of the full moon, and as the ebb had yet an hour and a half to run, I knew that our anchorage would be dry ground before slack water.

Mr. Taft's beds were three miles away, and for a long time we rowed silently in the wake of the other boats, once in a while grounding and our oar blades constantly striking bottom. At last we came upon soft mud covered with not more than two inches of water — not enough to float the boats. But the pirates at once were over the side, and by pushing and pulling on the flat-bottomed skiffs, we moved steadily along.

The full moon was partly obscured by high-flying clouds, but the pirates went their way with the familiarity born of long practice. After half a mile of the mud, we came upon a deep channel, up which we rowed, with dead oyster shoals looming high and dry on either side. At last we reached the picking grounds. Two men, on one of the shoals, hailed us and warned us off. But the Centipede, the Porpoise, Barchi, and Skilling took the lead, and followed by the rest of us, at least thirty men in half as many boats, rowed right up to the watchmen.

"You'd better slide outa this here," Barchi said threateningly, "or we'll fill you so full of holes you wouldn't float in molasses."

The watchmen wisely retreated before so overwhelming a force, and rowed their boat along the channel toward where the shore should be. Besides, it was in the plan for them to retreat.

We hauled the noses of the boats up on the shore side of a big shoal, and all hands, with sacks, spread out and began picking. Every now and again the clouds thinned before the face of the moon, and we could see the big oysters quite distinctly. In almost no time sacks were filled and carried back to the boats, where fresh ones were obtained. Nicholas and I returned often and anxiously to the boats with our little loads, but always found some one of the pirates coming or going.

"Never mind," he said; "no hurry. As they pick farther and farther away, it will take too long to carry to the boats. Then they'll stand the full sacks on end and pick them up when the tide comes in and the skiffs will float to them."

Fully half an hour went by, and the tide had begun to flood, when this came to pass. Leaving the pirates at their work, we stole back to the boats. One by one, and noiselessly, we shoved them off and made them fast in an awkward flotilla. Just as we were shoving off the last skiff, our own, one of the men came upon us. It was Barchi. His quick eye took in the situation at a glance, and he sprang for us; but we went clear with a mighty shove, and he was left floundering in the water over his head. As soon as he got back to the shoal he raised his voice and gave the alarm.

We rowed with all our strength, but it was slow going with so many boats in tow. A pistol cracked from the shoal, a second, and a third; then a regular fusillade began. The bullets spat and spat all about us; but thick clouds had covered the moon, and in the dim darkness it was no more than random firing. It was only by chance that we could be hit.

"Wish we had a little steam launch," I panted.

"I'd just as soon the moon stayed hidden," Nicholas panted back.

It was slow work, but every stroke carried us farther away from the shoal and nearer the shore, till at last the shooting died down, and when the moon did come out we were too far away to be in danger. Not long afterward we answered a shoreward hail, and two Whitehall boats, each pulled by three pairs of oars, darted up to us. Charley's welcome face bent over to us, and he gripped us by the hands while he cried, "Oh, you joys! You joys! Both of you!"

When the flotilla had been landed, Nicholas and I and a watchman rowed out in one of the Whitehalls, with Charley in the stern-sheets. Two other Whitehalls followed us, and as the moon now shone brightly, we easily made out the oyster pirates on their lonely shoal. As we drew closer, they fired a rattling volley from their revolvers, and we promptly retreated beyond range.

"Lot of time," Charley said. "The flood is setting in fast, and by the time it's up to their necks there won't be any fight left in them."

So we lay on our oars and waited for the tide to do its work. This was the predicament of the pirates: because of the big run-out, the tide was now rushing back like a mill-race, and it was impossible for the strongest swimmer in the world to make against it the three miles to the sloops. Between the pirates and the shore were we, precluding escape in that direction. On the other hand, the water was rising rapidly over the shoals, and it was only a question of a few hours when it would be over their heads.

It was beautifully calm, and in the brilliant white moonlight we watched them through our night glasses and told Charley of the voyage of the *Coal Tar Maggie*. One o'clock came, and two o'clock, and the pirates were clustering on the highest shoal, waist-deep in water.

"Now this illustrates the value of imagination," Charley was saying. "Taft has been trying for years to get them, but he went at it with bull strength and failed. Now we used our heads . . ."

Just then I heard a scarcely audible gurgle of water, and holding up my hand for silence, I turned and pointed to a ripple slowly widening out in a growing circle. It was not more than fifty feet from us. We kept perfectly quiet and waited. After a minute the water broke six feet away, and a black head and white shoulder showed in the moonlight. With a snort of surprise and of suddenly expelled breath, the head and shoulder went down.

We pulled ahead several strokes and drifted with the current. Four pairs of eyes searched the surface of the water, but never another ripple showed, and never another glimpse did we catch of the black head and white shoulder.

"It's the Porpoise," Nicholas said. "It would take broad daylight for us to catch him."

At a quarter to three the pirates gave their first sign of weakening. We heard cries for help, in the unmistakable voice of the Centipede, and this time, on rowing closer, we were not fired upon. The Centipede was in a truly perilous plight. Only the heads and shoulders of his fellow-marauders showed above the water as they braced themselves against the current, while his feet were off the bottom and they were supporting him.

"Now, lads," Charley said briskly, "we have got you, and you can't get away. If you cut up rough, we'll have to leave you alone and the water will finish you.

But if you're good, we'll take you aboard, one man at a time, and you'll all be saved. What do you say ?"

"Ay," they chorused hoarsely between their chattering teeth.

"Then one man at a time, and the short men first."

The Centipede was the first to be pulled aboard, and he came willingly, though he objected when the constable put the handcuffs on him. Barchi was next hauled in, quite meek and resigned from his soaking. When we had ten in our boat we drew back, and the second Whitehall was loaded. The third Whitehall received nine prisoners only — a catch of twenty-nine in all.

"You didn't get the Porpoise," the Centipede said exultantly, as though his escape materially diminished our success.

Charley laughed. "But we saw him just

the same, a-snorting for shore like a puffing pig."

It was a mild and shivering band of pirates that we marched up the beach to the oyster house. In answer to Charley's knock, the door was flung open, and a pleasant wave of warm air rushed out upon us.

"You can dry your clothes here, lads, and get some hot coffee," Charley announced, as they filed in.

And there, sitting ruefully by the fire, with a steaming mug in his hand, was the Porpoise. With one accord Nicholas and I looked at Charley. He laughed gleefully.

"That comes of imagination," he said. "When you see a thing, you've got to see it all around, or what's the good of seeing it at all? I saw the beach, so I left a couple of constables behind to keep an eye on it. That's all."

IV

THE SIEGE OF THE "LAN-CASHIRE QUEEN"

THE SIEGE OF THE "LAN-CASHIRE QUEEN"

POSSIBLY our most exasperating experience on the fish patrol was when Charley Le Grant and I laid a two weeks' siege to a big four-masted English ship. Before we had finished with the affair, it became a pretty mathematical problem, and it was by the merest chance that we came into possession of the instrument that brought it to a successful termination.

After our raid on the oyster pirates we had returned to Oakland, where two more weeks passed before Neil Partington's wife was out of danger and on the highroad to recovery. So it was after an absence of a month, all told, that we turned the *Rein-*

deer's nose toward Benicia. When the cat's
away the mice will play, and in these four
weeks the fishermen had become very bold
in violating the law. When we passed
Point Pedro we noticed many signs of ac-
tivity among the shrimp-catchers, and, well
into San Pablo Bay, we observed a widely
scattered fleet of Upper Bay fishing-boats
hastily pulling in their nets and getting up
sail.

This was suspicious enough to warrant
investigation, and the first and only boat we
succeeded in boarding proved to have an
illegal net. The law permitted no smaller
mesh for catching shad than one that measured seven and one-half inches inside the
knots, while the mesh of this particular
net measured only three inches. It was a
flagrant breach of the rules, and the two
fishermen were forthwith put under arrest.

Neil Partington took one of them with him to help manage the *Reindeer*, while Charley and I went on ahead with the other in the captured boat.

But the shad fleet had headed over toward the Petaluma shore in wild flight, and for the rest of the run through San Pablo Bay we saw no more fishermen at all. Our prisoner, a bronzed and bearded Greek, sat sullenly on his net while we sailed his craft. It was a new Columbia River salmon boat, evidently on its first trip, and it handled splendidly. Even when Charley praised it, our prisoner refused to speak or to notice us, and we soon gave him up as a most unsociable fellow.

We ran up the Carquinez Straits and edged into the bight at Turner's Shipyard for smoother water. Here were lying several English steel sailing ships, waiting for

the wheat harvest; and here, most unexpectedly, in the precise place where we
had captured Big Alec, we came upon two
Italians in a skiff that was loaded with a
complete "Chinese" sturgeon line. The surprise was mutual, and we were on top of
them before either they or we were aware.
Charley had barely time to luff into the
wind and run up to them. I ran forward
and tossed them a line with orders to make
it fast. One of the Italians took a turn with
it over a cleat, while I hastened to lower our
big spritsail. This accomplished, the salmon
boat dropped astern, dragging heavily on
the skiff.

Charley came forward to board the prize,
but when I proceeded to haul alongside by
means of the line, the Italians cast it off.
We at once began drifting to leeward, while
they got out two pairs of oars and rowed

their light craft directly into the wind. This manœuvre for the moment disconcerted us, for in our large and heavily loaded boat we could not hope to catch them with the oars. But our prisoner came unexpectedly to our aid. His black eyes were flashing eagerly, and his face was flushed with suppressed excitement, as he dropped the centreboard, sprang forward with a single leap, and put up the sail.

"I've always heard that Greeks don't like Italians," Charley laughed, as he ran aft to the tiller.

And never in my experience have I seen a man so anxious for the capture of another as was our prisoner in the chase that followed. His eyes fairly snapped, and his nostrils quivered and dilated in a most extraordinary way. Charley steered while he tended the sheet; and though Charley was as quick and alert as a cat, the Greek could hardly control his impatience.

The Italians were cut off from the shore, which was fully a mile away at its nearest point. Did they attempt to make it, we could haul after them with the wind abeam, and overtake them before they had covered an eighth of the distance. But they were too wise to attempt it, contenting themselves with rowing lustily to windward along the starboard side of a big ship, the *Lancashire Queen*. But beyond the ship lay an open stretch of fully two miles to the shore in that direction. This, also, they dared not attempt, for we were bound to catch them before they could cover it. So, when they reached the bow of the *Lancashire Queen*, nothing remained but to pass around and row down her port side toward the stern, which meant rowing to leeward and giving us the advantage.

We in the salmon boat, sailing close on the wind, tacked about and crossed the ship's bow. Then Charley put up the tiller and headed down the port side of the ship, the Greek letting out the sheet and grinning with delight. The Italians were already half-way down the ship's length; but the stiff breeze at our back drove us after them far faster than they could row. Closer and closer we came, and I, lying down forward, was just reaching out to grasp the skiff, when it ducked under the great stern of the *Lancashire Queen.*

The chase was virtually where it had begun. The Italians were rowing up the starboard side of the ship, and we were hauled close on the wind and slowly edging out from the ship as we worked to windward. Then they darted around her bow and began the row down her port side, and we tacked about, crossed her bow, and went plunging down the wind hot after them. And again, just as I was reaching for the skiff, it ducked under the ship's stern and out of danger. And so it went, around and around, the skiff each time just barely ducking into safety.

By this time the ship's crew had become aware of what was taking place, and we could see their heads in a long row as they looked at us over the bulwarks. Each time we missed the skiff at the stern, they set up a wild cheer and dashed across to the other side of the *Lancashire Queen* to see the chase to windward. They showered us and the Italians with jokes and advice, and made our Greek so angry that at least once on each circuit he raised his fist and shook it at them in a rage. They came to look for this, and at each display greeted it with uproarious mirth.

"Wot a circus!" cried one.

"Tork about yer marine hippodromes, — if this ain't one, I'd like to know!" affirmed another.

"Six-days-go-as-yer-please," announced a third. "Who says the dagoes won't win?"

On the next tack to windward the Greek offered to change places with Charley.

"Let-a me sail-a de boat," he demanded. "I fix-a them, I catch-a them, sure."

This was a stroke at Charley's professional pride, for pride himself he did upon his boat-sailing abilities; but he yielded the tiller to the prisoner and took his place at the sheet. Three times again we made the circuit, and the Greek found that he could get no more speed out of the salmon boat than Charley had.

"Better give it up," one of the sailors advised from above.

The Greek scowled ferociously and shook his fist in his customary fashion. In the meanwhile my mind had not been idle, and I had finally evolved an idea.

"Keep going, Charley, one time more," I said.

And as we laid out on the next tack to windward, I bent a piece of line to a small grappling hook I had seen lying in the bail-hole. The end of the line I made fast to the ring-bolt in the bow, and with the hook out of sight I waited for the next opportunity to use it. Once more they made their leeward pull down the port side of the *Lancashire Queen*, and more once we churned down after them before the wind. Nearer and nearer we drew, and I was making believe to reach for them as before. The stern of the skiff was not six feet away, and they were laughing at me derisively as they ducked under the ship's stern. At that instant I suddenly arose and threw the grappling iron. It caught fairly and squarely on the rail of the skiff, which was jerked backward out of safety as the rope tautened and the salmon boat ploughed on.

A groan went up from the row of sailors above, which quickly changed to a cheer as one of the Italians whipped out a long sheath-knife and cut the rope. But we had drawn them out of safety, and Charley, from his place in the stern-sheets, reached over and clutched the stern of the skiff. The whole thing happened in a second of time, for the first Italian was cutting the rope and Charley was clutching the skiff, when the second Italian dealt him a rap over the head with an oar. Charley released his hold and collapsed, stunned, into the bottom of the salmon boat, and the Italians bent to their oars and escaped back under the ship's stern.

The Greek took both tiller and sheet and continued the chase around the *Lancashire Queen*, while I attended to Charley, on whose head a nasty lump was rapidly rising. Our sailor audience was wild with delight, and to a man encouraged the fleeing Italians. Charley sat up, with one hand on his head, and gazed about him sheepishly.

"It will never do to let them escape now," he said, at the same time drawing his revolver.

On our next circuit, he threatened the Italians with the weapon; but they rowed on stolidly, keeping splendid stroke and utterly disregarding him.

"If you don't stop, I'll shoot," Charley said menacingly.

" I suddenly arose and threw the grappling iron."

But this had no effect, nor were they to be frightened into surrendering even when he fired several shots dangerously close to them. It was too much to expect him to shoot unarmed men, and this they knew as well as we did; so they continued to pull doggedly round and round the ship.

"We'll run them down, then!" Charley exclaimed. "We'll wear them out and wind them!"

So the chase continued. Twenty times more we ran them around the *Lancashire Queen*, and at last we could see that even their iron muscles were giving out. They were nearly exhausted, and it was only a matter of a few more circuits, when the game took on a new feature. On the row to windward they always gained on us, so that they were half-way down the ship's side on the row to leeward when we were passing the bow. But this last time, as we passed the bow, we saw them escaping up the ship's gangway, which had been suddenly lowered. It was an organized move on the part of the sailors, evidently countenanced by the captain; for by the time we arrived where the gangway had been, it was being hoisted up, and the skiff, slung in the ship's davits, was likewise flying aloft out of reach.

The parley that followed with the captain was short and snappy. He absolutely forbade us to board the *Lancashire Queen*, and as absolutely refused to give up the two men. By this time Charley was as enraged as the Greek. Not only had he been foiled in a long and ridiculous chase, but he had been knocked senseless into the bottom of his boat by the men who had escaped him.

"Knock off my head with little apples," he declared emphatically, striking the fist of one hand into the palm of the other, "if those two men ever escape me! I'll stay here to get them if it takes the rest of my natural life, and if I don't get them, then I promise you I'll live unnaturally long or until I do get them, or my name's not Charley Le Grant!"

And then began the siege of the *Lancashire Queen*, a siege memorable in the annals of both fishermen and fish patrol. When the *Reindeer* came along, after a fruitless pursuit of the shad fleet, Charley instructed Neil Partington to send out his own salmon boat, with blankets, provisions, and a fisherman's charcoal stove. By sunset this exchange of boats was made, and we said good-by to our Greek, who perforce had to go into Benicia and be locked up for his own violation of the law. After supper, Charley and I kept alternate four-hour watches till daylight. The fishermen made no attempt to escape that night, though the ship sent out a boat for scouting purposes to find if the coast were clear.

By the next day we saw that a steady siege was in order, and we perfected our plans with an eye to our own comfort. A dock, known as the Solano Wharf, which ran out from the Benicia shore, helped us in this. It happened that the *Lancashire Queen*, the shore at Turner's Shipyard, and the Solano Wharf were the corners of a big equilateral triangle. From ship to shore, the side of the triangle along which the Italians had to escape, was a distance equal to that from the Solano Wharf to the shore, the side of the triangle along which we had to travel to get to the shore before the Italians. But as we could sail much faster than they could row, we could permit them to travel about half their side of the triangle before we darted out along our side. If we allowed them to get more than half-way, they were certain to beat us to shore; while if we started before they were half-way, they were equally certain to beat us back to the ship.

We found that an imaginary line, drawn from the end of the wharf to a windmill farther along the shore, cut precisely in half the line of the triangle along which the Italians must escape to reach the land. This line made it easy for us to determine how far to let them run away before we bestirred ourselves in pursuit. Day after day we would watch them through our glasses as they rowed leisurely along toward the half-way point; and as they drew close into line with the windmill, we would leap into the boat and get up sail. At sight of our preparation, they would turn and row slowly back to the *Lancashire Queen*, secure in the knowledge that we could not overtake them.

To guard against calms — when our salmon boat would be useless — we also had in readiness a light rowing skiff equipped with spoon-oars. But at such times, when the wind failed us, we were forced to row out from the wharf as soon as they rowed from the ship. In the nighttime, on the other hand, we were compelled to patrol the immediate vicinity of the ship; which we did, Charley and I standing four-hour watches turn and turn about. The Italians, however, preferred the daytime in which to escape, and so our long night vigils were without result.

"What makes me mad," said Charley, "is our being kept from our honest beds while those rascally lawbreakers are sleeping soundly every night. But much good may it do them," he threatened. "I'll keep them on that ship till the captain charges them board, as sure as a sturgeon's not a catfish!"

It was a tantalizing problem that confronted us. As long as we were vigilant, they could not escape; and as long as they were careful, we would be unable to catch them. Charley cudgelled his brains continually, but for once his imagination failed him. It was a problem apparently without other solution than that of patience. It was a waiting game, and whichever waited the longer was bound to win. To add to our irritation, friends of the Italians established a code of signals with them from the shore, so that we never dared relax the siege for a moment. And besides this, there were always one or two suspicious-looking fishermen hanging around the Solano Wharf and keeping watch on our actions. We could do nothing but "grin and bear it," as Charley said, while it took up all our time and prevented us from doing other work.

The days went by, and there was no change in the situation. Not that no attempts were made to change it. One night friends from the shore came out in a skiff and attempted to confuse us while the two Italians escaped. That they did not succeed was due to the lack of a little oil on the ship's davits. For we were drawn back from the pursuit of the strange boat by the creaking of the davits, and arrived at the *Lancashire Queen* just as the Italians were lowering their skiff. Another night, fully half a dozen skiffs rowed around us in the darkness, but we held on like a leech to the side of the ship and frustrated their plan till they grew angry and showered us with abuse. Charley laughed to himself in the bottom of the boat.

"It's a good sign, lad," he said to me. "When men begin to abuse, make sure they're losing patience; and shortly after they lose patience, they lose their heads. Mark my words, if we only hold out, they'll get careless some fine day, and then we'll get them."

But they did not grow careless, and Charley confessed that this was one of the times when all signs failed. Their patience seemed equal to ours, and the second week of the siege dragged monotonously along. Then Charley's lagging imagination quickened sufficiently to suggest a ruse. Peter Boyelen, a new patrolman and one unknown to the fisher-folk, happened to arrive in Benicia, and we took him into our plan. We were as secret as possible about it, but in some unfathomable way the friends ashore got word to the beleaguered Italians to keep their eyes open.

On the night we were to put our ruse into effect, Charley and I took up our usual station in our rowing skiff alongside the *Lancashire Queen*. After it was thoroughly dark, Peter Boyelen came out in a crazy duck boat, the kind you can pick up and carry away under one arm. When we heard him coming along, paddling noisily, we slipped away a short distance into the darkness and rested on our oars. Opposite the gangway, having jovially hailed the anchor-watch of the *Lancashire Queen* and asked the direction of the *Scottish Chiefs*, another wheat ship, he awkwardly capsized himself. The man who was standing the anchor-watch ran down the gangway and hauled him out of the water. This was what he wanted, to get aboard the ship; and the next thing he expected was to be taken on deck and then below to warm up and dry out. But the captain inhospitably kept him perched on the lowest gangway step, shivering miserably and with his feet dangling in the water, till we, out of very pity, rowed in from the darkness and took him off. The jokes and gibes of the awakened crew sounded anything but sweet in our ears, and even the two Italians climbed up on the rail and laughed down at us long and maliciously.

"That's all right," Charley said in a low voice, which I only could hear. "I'm mighty glad it's not us that's laughing first. We'll save our laugh to the end, eh, lad?"

He clapped a hand on my shoulder as he finished, but it seemed to me that there was more determination than hope in his voice.

It would have been possible for us to secure the aid of United States marshals and board the English ship, backed by government authority. But the instructions of the Fish Commission were to the effect that the patrolmen should avoid complications, and this one, did we call on the higher powers, might well end in a pretty international tangle.

The second week of the siege drew to its close, and there was no sign of change in the situation. On the morning of the fourteenth day the change came, and it came in a guise as unexpected and startling to us as it was to the men we were striving to capture.

Charley and I, after our customary night vigil by the side of the *Lancashire Queen*, rowed into the Solano Wharf.

"Hello!" cried Charley, in surprise. "In the name of reason and common sense, what is that? Of all unmannerly craft did you ever see the like?"

Well might he exclaim, for there, tied up to the dock, lay the strangest-looking launch I had ever seen. Not that it could be called a launch, either, but it seemed to resemble a launch more than any other kind of boat. It was seventy feet long, but so narrow was it, and so bare of superstructure, that it appeared much smaller than it really was. It was built wholly of steel, and was painted black. Three smokestacks, a good distance apart and raking well aft, arose in single file amidships; while the bow, long and lean and sharp as a knife, plainly advertised that the boat was made for speed. Passing under the stern, we read *Streak*, painted in small white letters.

Charley and I were consumed with curiosity. In a few minutes we were on board and talking with an engineer who was watching the sunrise from the deck. He was quite willing to satisfy our curiosity, and in a few minutes we learned that the *Streak* had come in after dark from San Francisco; that this was what might be called the trial trip; and that she was the property of Silas Tate, a young mining millionaire of California, whose fad was high-speed yachts. There was some talk about turbine engines, direct application of steam, and the absence of pistons, rods, and cranks,—all of which was beyond me, for

I was familiar only with sailing craft; but I did understand the last words of the engineer.

"Four thousand horse-power and forty-five miles an hour, though you wouldn't think it," he concluded proudly.

"Say it again, man! Say it again!" Charley exclaimed in an excited voice.

"Four thousand horse-power and forty-five miles an hour," the engineer repeated, grinning good-naturedly.

"Where's the owner?" was Charley's next question. "Is there any way I can speak to him?"

The engineer shook his head. "No, I'm afraid not. He's asleep, you see."

At that moment a young man in blue uniform came on deck farther aft and stood regarding the sunrise.

"There he is, that's him, that's Mr. Tate," said the engineer.

Charley walked aft and spoke to him, and while he talked earnestly the young man listened with an amused expression on his face. He must have inquired about the depth of water close in to the shore at Turner's Shipyard, for I could see Charley making gestures and explaining. A few minutes later he came back in high glee.

"Come on, lad," he said. "On to the dock with you. We've got them!"

It was our good fortune to leave the *Streak* when we did, for a little later one of the spy fishermen appeared. Charley and I took up our accustomed places, on the stringer-piece, a little ahead of the *Streak* and over our own boat, where we could comfortably watch the *Lancashire Queen*. Nothing occurred till about nine o'clock, when we saw the two Italians leave the ship and pull along their side of the triangle

toward the shore. Charley looked as un-
concerned as could be, but before they had
covered a quarter of the distance, he whispered to me:

"Forty-five miles an hour . . . nothing
can save them . . . . they are ours!"

Slowly the two men rowed along till they
were nearly in line with the windmill. This
was the point where we always jumped
into our salmon boat and got up the sail,
and the two men, evidently expecting it,
seemed surprised when we gave no sign.

When they were directly in line with the
windmill, as near to the shore as to the
ship, and nearer the shore than we had ever
allowed them before, they grew suspicious.
We followed them through the glasses, and
saw them standing up in the skiff and trying
to find out what we were doing. The spy
fisherman, sitting beside us on the stringer-

piece, was likewise puzzled. He could not understand our inactivity. The men in the skiff rowed nearer the shore, but stood up again and scanned it, as if they thought we might be in hiding there. But a man came out on the beach and waved a handkerchief to indicate that the coast was clear. That settled them. They bent to the oars to make a dash for it. Still Charley waited. Not until they had covered three-quarters of the distance from the *Lancashire Queen*, which left them hardly more than a quarter of a mile to gain the shore, did Charley slap me on the shoulder and cry:

"They're ours! They're ours!"

We ran the few steps to the side of the *Streak* and jumped aboard. Stern and bow lines were cast off in a jiffy. The *Streak* shot ahead and away from the wharf. The spy fisherman we had left behind on the stringer-piece pulled out a revolver and fired five shots into the air in rapid succession. The men in the skiff gave instant heed to the warning, for we could see them pulling away like mad.

But if they pulled like mad, I wonder how our progress can be described? We fairly flew. So frightful was the speed with which we displaced the water, that a wave rose up on either side our bow and foamed aft in a series of three stiff, up-standing waves, while astern a great crested billow pursued us hungrily, as though at each moment it would fall aboard and destroy us. The *Streak* was pulsing and vibrating and roaring like a thing alive. The wind of our progress was like a gale — a forty-five-mile gale. We could not face it and draw breath without choking and strangling. It blew the smoke straight back from the mouths of the smoke-stacks at a direct right angle to the perpendicular. In fact, we were travelling as fast as an express train. "We just *streaked* it," was the way Charley told it afterward, and I think his description comes nearer than any I can give.

As for the Italians in the skiff — hardly had we started, it seemed to me, when we were on top of them. Naturally, we had to slow down long before we got to them; but even then we shot past like a whirlwind and were compelled to circle back between them and the shore. They had rowed steadily, rising from the thwarts at every stroke, up to the moment we passed them, when they recognized Charley and me. That took the last bit of fight out of them. They hauled in their oars and sullenly submitted to arrest.

"Well, Charley," Neil Partington said, as we discussed it on the wharf afterward, "I fail to see where your boasted imagination came into play this time."

But Charley was true to his hobby. "Imagination?" he demanded, pointing to the *Streak*. "Look at that! Just look at it! If the invention of that isn't imagination, I should like to know what is.

"Of course," he added, "it's the other fellow's imagination, but it did the work all the same."

V

CHARLEY'S COUP

CHARLEY'S COUP

PERHAPS our most laughable exploit on the fish patrol, and at the same time our most dangerous one, was when we rounded in, at a single haul, an even score of wrathful fishermen. Charley called it a "coop," having heard Neil Partington use the term; but I think he misunderstood the word, and thought it meant "coop," to catch, to trap. The fishermen, however, coup or coop, must have called it a Waterloo, for it was the severest stroke ever dealt them by the fish patrol, while they had invited it by open and impudent defiance of the law.

During what is called the "open season" the fishermen might catch as many salmon as their luck allowed and their boats could hold. But there was one important restriction. From sun-down Saturday night to sun-up Monday morning, they were not permitted to set a net. This was a wise provision on the part of the Fish Commission, for it was necessary to give the spawning salmon some opportunity to ascend the river and lay their eggs. And this law, with only an occasional violation, had been obediently observed by the Greek fishermen who caught salmon for the canneries and the market.

One Sunday morning, Charley received a telephone call from a friend in Collinsville, who told him that the full force of fishermen was out with its nets. Charley and I jumped into our salmon boat and started for the scene of the trouble. With a light favoring wind at our back we went through the Carquinez Straits, crossed Suisun Bay, passed the Ship Island Light, and came upon the whole fleet at work.

But first let me describe the method by which they worked. The net used is what is known as a gill-net. It has a simple diamond-shaped mesh which measures at least seven and one-half inches between the knots. From five to seven and even eight hundred feet in length, these nets are only a few feet wide. They are not stationary, but float with the current, the upper edge supported on the surface by floats, the lower edge sunk by means of leaden weights.

This arrangement keeps the net upright in the current and effectually prevents all but the smaller fish from ascending the river. The salmon, swimming near the surface, as is their custom, run their heads through these meshes, and are prevented from going on through by their larger girth of body, and from going back because of their gills, which catch in the mesh. It requires two fishermen to set such a net, — one to row the boat, while the other, standing in the stern, carefully pays out the net. When it is all out, stretching directly across the stream, the men make their boat fast to one end of the net and drift along with it.

As we came upon the fleet of law-breaking fishermen, each boat two or three hundred yards from its neighbors, and boats and nets dotting the river as far as we could see, Charley said:

"I've only one regret, lad, and that is that I haven't a thousand arms so as to be able to catch them all. As it is, we'll only be able to catch one boat, for while we are tackling that one it will be up nets and away with the rest."

As we drew closer, we observed none of

the usual flurry and excitement which our appearance invariably produced. Instead, each boat lay quietly by its net, while the fishermen favored us with not the slightest attention.

"It's curious," Charley muttered. "Can it be they don't recognize us?"

I said that it was impossible, and Charley agreed; yet there was a whole fleet, manned by men who knew us only too well, and who took no more notice of us than if we were a hay scow or a pleasure yacht.

This did not continue to be the case, however, for as we bore down upon the nearest net, the men to whom it belonged detached their boat and rowed slowly toward the shore. The rest of the boats showed no sign of uneasiness.

"That's funny," was Charley's remark. "But we can confiscate the net, at any rate."

We lowered sail, picked up one end of the net, and began to heave it into the boat. But at the first heave we heard a bullet zip-zipping past us on the water, followed by the faint report of a rifle. The men who had rowed ashore were shooting at us. At the next heave a second bullet went zipping past, perilously near. Charley took a turn around a pin and sat down. There were no more shots. But as soon as he began to heave in, the shooting recommenced.

"That settles it," he said, flinging the end of the net overboard. "You fellows want it worse than we do, and you can have it."

We rowed over toward the next net, for Charley was intent on finding out whether or not we were face to face with an organized defiance. As we approached, the two fishermen proceeded to cast off from their net and row ashore, while the first two rowed back and made fast to the net we had abandoned. And at the second net we were greeted by rifle shots till we desisted and went on to the third, where the manœuvre was again repeated.

Then we gave it up, completely routed, and hoisted sail and started on the long windward beat back to Benicia. A number of Sundays went by, on each of which the law was persistently violated. Yet, short of an armed force of soldiers, we could do nothing. The fishermen had hit upon a new idea and were using it for all it was worth, while there seemed no way by which we could get the better of them.

About this time Neil Partington happened along from the Lower Bay, where he had been for a number of weeks. With him was Nicholas, the Greek boy who had helped us in our raid on the oyster pirates, and the pair of them took a hand. We made our arrangements carefully. It was planned that while Charley and I tackled the nets, they were to be hidden ashore so as to ambush the fishermen who landed to shoot at us.

It was a pretty plan. Even Charley said it was. But we reckoned not half so well as the Greeks. They forestalled us by ambushing Neil and Nicholas and taking them prisoners, while, as of old, bullets whistled about our ears when Charley and I attempted to take possession of the nets. When we were again beaten off, Neil Partington and Nicholas were released. They were rather shamefaced when they put in an appearance, and Charley chaffed them unmercifully. But Neil chaffed back, demanding to know why Charley's imagination had not long since overcome the difficulty.

" Just you wait; the idea'll come all right," Charley promised.

"Most probably," Neil agreed. "But I'm afraid the salmon will be exterminated first, and then there will be no need for it when it does come."

Neil Partington, highly disgusted with his adventure, departed for the Lower Bay, taking Nicholas with him, and Charley and I were left to our own resources. This meant that the Sunday fishing would be left to itself, too, until such time as Charley's idea happened along. I puzzled my head a good deal to find out some way of checkmating the Greeks, as also did Charley, and we broached a thousand expedients which on discussion proved worthless.

The fishermen, on the other hand, were in high feather, and their boasts went up and down the river to add to our discomfiture. Among all classes of them we became aware of a growing insubordination. We were beaten, and they were losing respect for us. With the loss of respect, contempt began to arise. Charley began to be spoken of as the "olda woman," and I received my rating as the "pee-wee kid." The situation was fast becoming unbearable, and we knew that we should have to deliver a stunning stroke at the Greeks in order to regain the old-time respect in which we had stood.

Then one morning the idea came. We were down on Steamboat Wharf, where the river steamers made their landings, and where we found a group of amused long-shore-men and loafers listening to the hard-luck tale of a sleepy-eyed young fellow in long sea-boots. He was a sort of amateur fish-erman, he said, fishing for the local market of Berkeley. Now Berkeley was on the Lower Bay, thirty miles away. On the previous night, he said, he had set his net and dozed off to sleep in the bottom of the boat.

The next he knew it was morning, and he opened his eyes to find his boat rubbing softly against the piles of Steamboat Wharf at Benicia. Also he saw the river steamer *Apache* lying ahead of him, and a couple of deck-hands disentangling the shreds of his net from the paddle-wheel. In short, after he had gone to sleep, his fisherman's riding light had gone out, and the *Apache* had run over his net. Though torn pretty well to pieces, the net in some way still remained foul, and he had had a thirty-mile tow out of his course.

Charley nudged me with his elbow. I grasped his thought on the instant, but objected:

"We can't charter a steamboat."

"Don't intend to," he rejoined. "But

let's run over to Turner's Shipyard. I've something in my mind there that may be of use to us."

And over we went to the shipyard, where Charley led the way to the *Mary Rebecca*, lying hauled out on the ways, where she was being cleaned and overhauled. She was a scow-schooner we both knew well, carrying a cargo of one hundred and forty tons and a spread of canvas greater than any other schooner on the bay.

"How d'ye do, Ole," Charley greeted a big blue-shirted Swede who was greasing the jaws of the main gaff with a piece of pork rind.

Ole grunted, puffed away at his pipe, and went on greasing. The captain of a bay schooner is supposed to work with his hands just as well as the men.

Ole Ericsen verified Charley's conjecture

that the *Mary Rebecca*, as soon as launched, would run up the San Joaquin River nearly to Stockton for a load of wheat. Then Charley made his proposition, and Ole Ericsen shook his head.

"Just a hook, one good-sized hook," Charley pleaded.

"No, Ay tank not," said Ole Ericsen. "Der *Mary Rebecca* yust hang up on efery mud-bank with that hook. Ay don't want to lose der *Mary Rebecca*. She's all Ay got."

"No, no," Charley hurried to explain. "We can put the end of the hook through the bottom from the outside, and fasten it on the inside with a nut. After it's done its work, why, all we have to do is to go down into the hold, unscrew the nut, and out drops the hook. Then drive a wooden peg into the hole, and the *Mary Rebecca* will be all right again."

Ole Ericsen was obstinate for a long time; but in the end, after we had had dinner with him, he was brought round to consent.

"Ay do it, by Yupiter!" he said, striking one huge fist into the palm of the other hand. "But yust hurry you up with der hook.   Der *Mary Rebecca* slides into der water to-night."

It was Saturday, and Charley had need to hurry. We headed for the shipyard blacksmith shop, where, under Charley's directions, a most generously curved hook of heavy steel was made. Back we hastened to the *Mary Rebecca*. Aft of the great centreboard case, through what was properly her keel, a hole was bored.   The end of the hook was inserted from the outside, and Charley, on the inside, screwed the nut on tightly. As it stood complete, the hook projected over a foot beneath the bottom of the schooner. Its curve was something like the curve of a sickle, but deeper.

In the late afternoon the *Mary Rebecca* was launched, and preparations were finished for the start up-river next morning.   Charley and Ole intently studied the evening sky for signs of wind, for without a good breeze our project was doomed to failure. They agreed that there were all the signs of a stiff westerly wind — not the ordinary afternoon sea-breeze, but a half-gale, which even then was springing up.

Next morning found their predictions verified. The sun was shining brightly, but something more than a half-gale was shrieking up the Carquinez Straits, and the *Mary Rebecca* got under way with two reefs in her mainsail and one in her foresail. We found it quite rough in the Straits and in Suisun Bay; but as the water grew more land-locked it became calm, though without let-up in the wind.

Off Ship Island Light the reefs were shaken out, and at Charley's suggestion a big fisherman's staysail was made all ready for hoisting, and the maintopsail, bunched into a cap at the masthead, was overhauled so that it could be set on an instant's notice.

We were tearing along, wing-and-wing, before the wind, foresail to starboard and mainsail to port, as we came upon the salmon fleet. There they were, boats and nets, as on that first Sunday when they had bested us, strung out evenly over the river as far as we could see. A narrow space on the right-hand side of the channel was left clear for steamboats, but the rest of the river was covered with the wide-stretching nets. The narrow space was our logical course, but Charley, at the wheel, steered the *Mary Rebecca* straight for the nets.

This did not cause any alarm among the

fishermen, because up-river sailing craft are always provided with "shoes" on the ends of their keels, which permit them to slip over the nets without fouling them.

"Now she takes it!" Charley cried, as we dashed across the middle of a line of floats which marked a net. At one end of this line was a small barrel buoy, at the other the two fishermen in their boat. Buoy and boat at once began to draw together, and the fishermen to cry out, as they were jerked after us. A couple of minutes later we hooked a second net, and then a third, and in this fashion we tore straight up through the centre of the fleet.

The consternation we spread among the fishermen was tremendous. As fast as we hooked a net the two ends of it, buoy and boat, came together as they dragged out astern; and so many buoys and boats, coming together at such breakneck speed, kept the fishermen on the jump to avoid smashing into one another. Also, they shouted at us like mad to heave to into the wind, for they took it as some drunken prank on the part of scow-sailors, little dreaming that we were the fish patrol.

The drag of a single net is very heavy, and Charley and Ole Ericsen decided that even in such a wind ten nets were all the *Mary Rebecca* could take along with her. So when we had hooked ten nets, with ten boats containing twenty men streaming along behind us, we veered to the left out of the fleet and headed toward Collinsville.

We were all jubilant. Charley was handling the wheel as though he were steering the winning yacht home in a race. The two sailors who made up the crew of the *Mary Rebecca*, were grinning and joking. Ole

"The consternation we spread among the fishermen was
tremendous."

Ericsen was rubbing his huge hands in child-like glee.

"Ay tank you fish patrol fallers never ban so lucky as when you sail with Ole Ericsen," he was saying, when a rifle cracked sharply astern, and a bullet gouged along the newly painted cabin, glanced on a nail, and sang shrilly onward into space.

This was too much for Ole Ericsen. At sight of his beloved paintwork thus defaced, he jumped up and shook his fist at the fishermen; but a second bullet smashed into the cabin not six inches from his head, and he dropped down to the deck under cover of the rail.

All the fishermen had rifles, and they now opened a general fusillade. We were all driven to cover — even Charley, who was compelled to desert the wheel. Had it not been for the heavy drag of the nets, we would inevitably have broached to at the mercy of the enraged fishermen.   But the nets, fastened to the bottom of the *Mary Rebecca* well aft, held her stern into the wind, and she continued to plough on, though somewhat erratically.

Charley, lying on the deck, could just manage to reach the lower spokes of the wheel; but while he could steer after a fashion, it was very awkward.   Ole Ericsen bethought himself of a large piece of sheet steel in the empty hold.   It was in fact a plate from the side of the *New Jersey*, a steamer which had recently been wrecked outside the Golden Gate, and in the salving of which the *Mary Rebecca* had taken part.

Crawling carefully along the deck, the two sailors, Ole, and myself got the heavy plate on deck and aft, where we reared it as a shield between the wheel and the fishermen.

The bullets whanged and banged against it till it rang like a bull's-eye, but Charley grinned in its shelter, and coolly went on steering.

So we raced along, behind us a howling, screaming bedlam of wrathful Greeks, Collinsville ahead, and bullets spat-spatting all around us.

"Ole," Charley said in a faint voice, "I don't know what we're going to do."

Ole Ericsen, lying on his back close to the rail and grinning upward at the sky, turned over on his side and looked at him. "Ay tank we go into Collinsville yust der same," he said.

"But we can't stop," Charley groaned. "I never thought of it, but we can't stop."

A look of consternation slowly overspread Ole Ericsen's broad face. It was only too true. We had a hornet's nest on our hands, and to stop at Collinsville would be to have it about our ears.

" Every man Jack of them has a gun," one of the sailors remarked cheerfully.

" Yes, and a knife, too," the other sailor added.

It was Ole Ericsen's turn to groan. "What for a Svaidish faller like me monkey with none of my biziness, I don't know," he soliloquized.

A bullet glanced on the stern and sang off to starboard like a spiteful bee. " There's nothing to do but plump the *Mary Rebecca* ashore and run for it," was the verdict of the first cheerful sailor.

" And leaf der *Mary Rebecca?*" Ole demanded, with unspeakable horror in his voice.

"Not unless you want to," was the response. "But I don't want to be within a thousand miles of her when those fellers come aboard"

— indicating the bedlam of excited Greeks towing behind.

We were right in at Collinsville then, and went foaming by within biscuit-toss of the wharf.

"I only hope the wind holds out," Charley said, stealing a glance at our prisoners.

"What of der wind?" Ole demanded disconsolately. "Der river will not hold out, and then . . . and then . . ."

"It's head for tall timber, and the Greeks take the hindermost," adjudged the cheerful sailor, while Ole was stuttering over what would happen when we came to the end of the river.

We had now reached a dividing of the ways. To the left was the mouth of the Sacramento River, to the right the mouth of the San Joaquin. The cheerful sailor crept forward and jibed over the foresail as Charley put the helm to starboard and we swerved to the right into the San Joaquin. The wind, from which we had been running away on an even keel, now caught us on our beam, and the *Mary Rebecca* was pressed down on her port side as if she were about to capsize.

Still we dashed on, and still the fishermen dashed on behind. The value of their nets was greater than the fines they would have to pay for violating the fish laws; so to cast off from their nets and escape, which they could easily do, would profit them nothing. Further, they remained by their nets instinctively, as a sailor remains by his ship. And still further, the desire for vengeance was roused, and we could depend upon it that they would follow us to the ends of the earth, if we undertook to tow them that far.

The rifle-firing had ceased, and we looked astern to see what our prisoners were doing.

The boats were strung along at unequal distances apart, and we saw the four nearest ones bunching together. This was done by the boat ahead trailing a small rope astern to the one behind. When this was caught, they would cast off from their net and heave in on the line till they were brought up to the boat in front. So great was the speed at which we were travelling, however, that this was very slow work. Sometimes the men would strain to their utmost and fail to get in an inch of the rope; at other times they came ahead more rapidly.

When the four boats were near enough together for a man to pass from one to another, one Greek from each of three got into the nearest boat to us, taking his rifle with him. This made five in the foremost boat, and it was plain that their intention was to board us. This they undertook to do, by main strength and sweat, running hand over hand the float-line of a net. And though it was slow, and they stopped frequently to rest, they gradually drew nearer.

Charley smiled at their efforts, and said, "Give her the topsail, Ole."

The cap at the mainmast head was broken out, and sheet and downhaul pulled flat, amid a scattering rifle fire from the boats; and the *Mary Rebecca* lay over and sprang ahead faster than ever.

But the Greeks were undaunted. Unable, at the increased speed, to draw themselves nearer by means of their hands, they rigged from the blocks of their boat sail what sailors call a "watch-tackle." One of them, held by the legs by his mates, would lean far over the bow and make the tackle fast to the float-line. Then they would heave in on the tackle till the blocks were together, when the manœuvre would be repeated.

"Have to give her the staysail," Charley
said.

Ole Ericsen looked at the straining *Mary
Rebecca* and shook his head. "It will take
der masts out of her," he said.

"And we'll be taken out of her if you
don't," Charley replied.

Ole shot an anxious glance at his masts,
another at the boat load of armed Greeks,
and consented.

The five men were in the bow of the boat
— a bad place when a craft is towing. I was
watching the behavior of their boat as the
great fisherman's staysail, far, far larger
than the topsail and used only in light
breezes, was broken out. As the *Mary
Rebecca* lurched forward with a tremendous
jerk, the nose of the boat ducked down into
the water, and the men tumbled over one
another in a wild rush into the stern to save

the boat from being dragged sheer under water.

"That settles them!" Charley remarked, though he was anxiously studying the behavior of the *Mary Rebecca*, which was being driven under far more canvas than she was rightly able to carry.

"Next stop is Antioch!" announced the cheerful sailor, after the manner of a railway conductor. "And next comes Merryweather!"

"Come here, quick," Charley said to me.

I crawled across the deck and stood upright beside him in the shelter of the sheet steel.

"Feel in my inside pocket," he commanded, "and get my notebook. That's right. Tear out a blank page and write what I tell you."

And this is what I wrote:

Telephone to Merryweather, to the sheriff, the constable, or the judge. Tell them we are coming and to turn out the town. Arm everybody. Have them down on the wharf to meet us or we are gone gooses.

"Now make it good and fast to that marlinspike, and stand by to toss it ashore."

I did as he directed. By then we were close to Antioch. The wind was shouting through our rigging, the *Mary Rebecca* was half over on her side and rushing ahead like an ocean greyhound. The seafaring folk of Antioch had seen us breaking out topsail and staysail, a most reckless performance in such weather, and had hurried to the wharf-ends in little groups to find out what was the matter.

Straight down the water front we boomed, Charley edging in till a man could almost leap ashore. When he gave the signal I tossed the marlinspike. It struck the planking of the wharf a resounding smash, bounced along fifteen or twenty feet, and was pounced upon by the amazed onlookers.

It all happened in a flash, for the next minute Antioch was behind and we were heeling it up the San Joaquin toward Merry-weather, six miles away. The river straightened out here into its general easterly course, and we squared away before the wind, wing-and-wing once more, the foresail bellying out to starboard.

Ole Ericsen seemed sunk into a state of stolid despair. Charley and the two sailors were looking hopeful, as they had good reason to be. Merryweather was a coal-mining town, and, it being Sunday, it was reasonable to expect the men to be in town. Further, the coal-miners had never lost any love for the Greek fishermen, and were pretty certain to render us hearty assistance.

We strained our eyes for a glimpse of the town, and the first sight we caught of it gave us immense relief. The wharves were black with men. As we came closer, we could see them still arriving, stringing down the main street, guns in their hands and on the run. Charley glanced astern at the fishermen with a look of ownership in his eye which till then had been missing. The Greeks were plainly overawed by the display of armed strength and were putting their own rifles away.

We took in topsail and staysail, dropped the main peak, and as we got abreast of the principal wharf jibed the mainsail. The *Mary Rebecca* shot around into the wind, the captive fishermen describing a great arc behind her, and forged ahead till she lost way, when lines were flung ashore and she was made fast. This was accomplished under a hurricane of cheers from the delighted miners.

Ole Ericsen heaved a great sigh. "Ay never tank Ay see my wife never again," he confessed.

"Why, we were never in any danger," said Charley.

Ole looked at him incredulously.

"Sure, I mean it," Charley went on. "All we had to do, any time, was to let go our end — as I am going to do now, so that those Greeks can untangle their nets."

He went below with a monkey-wrench, unscrewed the nut, and let the hook drop off. When the Greeks had hauled their nets into their boats and made everything ship-shape, a posse of citizens took them off our hands and led them away to jail.

"Ay tank Ay ban a great big fool," said Ole Ericsen. But he changed his mind when the admiring townspeople crowded aboard to shake hands with him, and a couple of enterprising newspaper men took photographs of the *Mary Rebecca* and her captain.

VI

DEMETRIOS CONTOS

DEMETRIOS CONTOS

IT must not be thought, from what I have told of the Greek fishermen, that they were altogether bad. Far from it. But they were rough men, gathered together in isolated communities and fighting with the elements for a livelihood. They lived far away from the law and its workings, did not understand it, and thought it tyranny. Especially did the fish laws seem tyrannical. And because of this, they looked upon the men of the fish patrol as their natural enemies.

We menaced their lives, or their living, which is the same thing, in many ways. We confiscated illegal traps and nets, the materials of which had cost them considerable sums and the making of which required weeks of labor. We prevented them from catching fish at many times and seasons, which was equivalent to preventing them from making as good a living as they might have made had we not been in existence. And when we captured them, they were brought into the courts of law, where heavy cash fines were collected from them. As a result, they hated us vindictively. As the dog is the natural enemy of the cat, the snake of man, so were we of the fish patrol the natural enemies of the fishermen.

But it is to show that they could act generously as well as hate bitterly that this story of Demetrios Contos is told. Demetrios Contos lived in Vallejo. Next to Big Alec, he was the largest, bravest, and most influential man among the Greeks. He had given us no trouble, and I doubt if he would ever have clashed with us had he not invested in a new salmon boat. This boat was the cause of all the trouble. He had had it built upon his own model, in which the lines of the general salmon boat were somewhat modified.

To his high elation he found his new boat very fast — in fact, faster than any other boat on the bay or rivers. Forthwith he grew proud and boastful: and, our raid with the *Mary Rebecca* on the Sunday salmon fishers having wrought fear in their hearts, he sent a challenge up to Benicia. One of the local fishermen conveyed it to us; it was to the effect that Demetrios Contos would sail up from Vallejo on the following Sunday, and in the plain sight of Benicia set his net and catch salmon, and that Charley Le Grant, patrolman, might come and get him if he could. Of course Charley and I had heard nothing of the new boat. Our own boat was pretty fast, and we were not afraid to have a brush with any other that happened along.

Sunday came. The challenge had been bruited abroad, and the fishermen and sea-faring folk of Benicia turned out to a man, crowding Steamboat Wharf till it looked like the grand stand at a football match. Charley and I had been sceptical, but the fact of the crowd convinced us that there was something in Demetrios Contos's dare.

In the afternoon, when the sea-breeze had picked up in strength, his sail hove into view as he bowled along before the wind. He tacked a score of feet from the wharf, waved his hand theatrically, like a knight about to enter the lists, received a hearty cheer in return, and stood away into the Straits for a couple of hundred yards. Then he lowered sail, and, drifting the boat sidewise by means of the wind, proceeded to set his net. He did not set much of it, possibly fifty feet; yet Charley and I were thunderstruck at the man's effrontery. We did not know at the time, but we learned afterward, that the net he used was old and worthless. It *could* catch fish, true; but a catch of any size would have torn it to pieces.

Charley shook his head and said:

"I confess, it puzzles me. What if he has out only fifty feet? He could never get it in if we once started for him. And why does he come here anyway, flaunting his law-breaking in our faces? Right in our home town, too."

Charley's voice took on an aggrieved tone, and he continued for some minutes to inveigh against the brazenness of Demetrios Contos.

In the meantime, the man in question was lolling in the stern of his boat and watching the net floats. When a large fish is meshed in a gill-net, the floats by their agitation advertise the fact. And they evidently advertised it to Demetrios, for he pulled in about a dozen feet of net, and held aloft for a moment, before he flung it into the bottom of the boat, a big, glistening salmon. It was greeted by the audience on the wharf with round after round of cheers. This was more than Charley could stand.

"Come on, lad," he called to me; and we lost no time jumping into our salmon boat and getting up sail.

The crowd shouted warning to Demetrios, and as we darted out from the wharf we saw him slash his worthless net clear with a long knife. His sail was all ready to go up, and a moment later it fluttered in the sunshine. He ran aft, drew in the sheet, and filled on the long tack toward the Contra Costa Hills.

By this time we were not more than thirty feet astern.   Charley was jubilant.   He knew our boat was fast, and he knew, further, that in fine sailing few men were his equals. He was confident that we should surely catch Demetrios, and I shared his confidence.   But somehow we did not seem to gain.

It was a pretty sailing breeze.   We were gliding sleekly through the water, but Demetrios was slowly sliding away from us.   And not only was he going faster, but he was eating into the wind a fraction of a point closer than we.   This was sharply impressed upon us when he went about under the Contra Costa Hills and passed us on the other tack fully one hundred feet dead to windward.

"Whew!" Charley exclaimed. "Either that boat is a daisy, or we've got a five-gallon coal-oil can fast to our keel!"

It certainly looked it one way or the other.

And by the time Demetrios made the Sonoma Hills, on the other side of the Straits, we were so hopelessly outdistanced that Charley told me to slack off the sheet, and we squared away for Benicia. The fishermen on Steamboat Wharf showered us with ridicule when we returned and tied up. Charley and I got out and walked away, feeling rather sheepish, for it is a sore stroke to one's pride when he thinks he has a good boat and knows how to sail it, and another man comes along and beats him.

Charley mooned over it for a couple of days; then word was brought to us, as before, that on the next Sunday Demetrios Contos would repeat his performance. Charley roused himself. He had our boat out of the water, cleaned and repainted its bottom, made a trifling alteration about the centreboard, overhauled the running gear, and sat

up nearly all of Saturday night sewing on a
new and much larger sail. So large did he
make it, in fact, that additional ballast was
imperative, and we stowed away nearly five
hundred extra pounds of old railroad iron
in the bottom of the boat.

Sunday came, and with it came Demetrios
Contos, to break the law defiantly in open
day. Again we had the afternoon sea-breeze,
and again Demetrios cut loose some forty or
more feet of his rotten net, and got up sail
and under way under our very noses. But he
had anticipated Charley's move, and his own
sail peaked higher than ever, while a whole
extra cloth had been added to the after
leech.

It was nip and tuck across to the Contra
Costa Hills, neither of us seeming to gain or
to lose. But by the time we had made the
return tack to the Sonoma Hills, we could see

that, while we footed it at about equal speed, Demetrios had eaten into the wind the least bit more than we. Yet Charley was sailing our boat as finely and delicately as it was possible to sail it, and getting more out of it than he ever had before.

Of course, he could have drawn his revolver and fired at Demetrios; but we had long since found it contrary to our natures to shoot at a fleeing man guilty of only a petty offence. Also a sort of tacit agreement seemed to have been reached between the patrolmen and the fishermen. If we did not shoot while they ran away, they, in turn, did not fight if we once laid hands on them. Thus Demetrios Contos ran away from us, and we did no more than try our best to overtake him; and, in turn, if our boat proved faster than his, or was sailed better, he would, we knew, make no resistance when we caught up with him.

With our large sails and the healthy breeze romping up the Carquinez Straits, we found that our sailing was what is called "ticklish." We had to be constantly on the alert to avoid a capsize, and while Charley steered I held the main-sheet in my hand with but a single turn round a pin, ready to let go at any moment. Demetrios, we could see, sailing his boat alone, had his hands full.

But it was a vain undertaking for us to attempt to catch him. Out of his inner consciousness he had evolved a boat that was better than ours. And though Charley sailed fully as well, if not the least bit better, the boat he sailed was not so good as the Greek's.

"Slack away the sheet," Charley commanded; and as our boat fell off before the wind, Demetrios's mocking laugh floated down to us.

Charley shook his head, saying, "It's no

use. Demetrios has the better boat. If he tries his performance again, we must meet it with some new scheme."

This time it was my imagination that came to the rescue.

"What's the matter," I suggested, on the Wednesday following, "with my chasing Demetrios in the boat next Sunday, while you wait for him on the wharf at Vallejo when he arrives?"

Charley considered it a moment and slapped his knee.

"A good idea! You're beginning to use that head of yours. A credit to your teacher, I must say."

"But you mustn't chase him too far," he went on, the next moment, "or he'll head out into San Pablo Bay instead of running home to Vallejo, and there I'll be, standing lonely on the wharf and waiting in vain for him to arrive."

On Thursday Charley registered an objection to my plan.

"Everybody'll know I've gone to Vallejo, and you can depend upon it that Demetrios will know, too. I'm afraid we'll have to give up the idea."

This objection was only too valid, and for the rest of the day I struggled under my disappointment. But that night a new way seemed to open to me, and in my eagerness I awoke Charley from a sound sleep.

"Well," he grunted, "what's the matter? House afire?"

"No," I replied, "but my head is. Listen to this. On Sunday you and I will be around Benicia up to the very moment Demetrios's sail heaves into sight. This will lull everybody's suspicions. Then, when Demetrios's sail does heave in sight, do you stroll leisurely away and up-town. All the fishermen will think you're beaten and that you know you're beaten."

"So far, so good," Charley commented, while I paused to catch breath.

"And very good indeed," I continued proudly. "You stroll carelessly up-town, but when you're once out of sight you leg it for all you're worth for Dan Maloney's. Take the little mare of his, and strike out on the county road for Vallejo. The road's in fine condition, and you can make it in quicker time than Demetrios can beat all the way down against the wind."

"And I'll arrange right away for the mare, first thing in the morning," Charley said, accepting the modified plan without hesitation.

"But, I say," he said, a little later, this time waking *me* out of a sound sleep.

I could hear him chuckling in the dark.

"I say, lad, isn't it rather a novelty for the fish patrol to be taking to horseback?"

"Imagination," I answered. "It's what you're always preaching — 'keep thinking one thought ahead of the other fellow, and you're bound to win out.'"

"He! he!" he chuckled. "And if one thought ahead, including a mare, doesn't take the other fellow's breath away this time, I'm not your humble servant, Charley Le Grant."

"But can you manage the boat alone?" he asked, on Friday. "Remember, we've a ripping big sail on her."

I argued my proficiency so well that he did not refer to the matter again till Saturday, when he suggested removing one whole cloth from the after leech. I guess it was the disappointment written on my face that made him desist; for I, also, had a pride in my

boat-sailing abilities, and I was almost wild
to get out alone with the big sail and go tearing down the Carquinez Straits in the wake
of the flying Greek.

As usual, Sunday and Demetrios Contos
arrived together. It had become the regular
thing for the fishermen to assemble on Steamboat Wharf to greet his arrival and to laugh
at our discomfiture. He lowered sail a
couple of hundred yards out and set his customary fifty feet of rotten net.

"I suppose this nonsense will keep up as
long as his old net holds out," Charley
grumbled, with intention, in the hearing of
several of the Greeks.

"Den I give-a heem my old-a net-a," one of
them spoke up, promptly and maliciously.

"I don't care," Charley answered. "I've
got some old net myself he can have — if he'll
come around and ask for it."

They all laughed at this, for they could afford to be sweet-tempered with a man so badly outwitted as Charley was.

"Well, so long, lad," Charley called to me a moment later. "I think I'll go up-town to Maloney's."

"Let me take the boat out?" I asked.

"If you want to," was his answer, as he turned on his heel and walked slowly away.

Demetrios pulled two large salmon out of his net, and I jumped into the boat. The fishermen crowded around in a spirit of fun, and when I started to get up sail overwhelmed me with all sorts of jocular advice. They even offered extravagant bets to one another that I would surely catch Demetrios, and two of them, styling themselves the committee of judges, gravely asked permission to come along with me to see how I did it.

But I was in no hurry. I waited to give

Charley all the time I could, and I pretended dissatisfaction with the stretch of the sail and slightly shifted the small tackle by which the huge sprit forces up the peak.   It was not until I was sure that Charley had reached Dan Maloney's and was on the little mare's back, that I cast off from the wharf and gave the big sail to the wind.   A stout puff filled it and suddenly pressed the lee gunwale down till a couple of buckets of water came inboard. A little thing like this will happen to the best small-boat sailors, and yet, though I instantly let go the sheet and righted, I was cheered sarcastically, as though I had been guilty of a very awkward blunder.

When Demetrios saw only one person in the fish patrol boat, and that one a boy, he proceeded to play with me.   Making a short tack out, with me not thirty feet behind, **he** returned, with his sheet a little free, to Steamboat Wharf. And there he made short tacks, and turned and twisted and ducked around, to the great delight of his sympathetic audience. I was right behind him all the time, and I dared to do whatever he did, even when he squared away before the wind and jibed his big sail over — a most dangerous trick with such a sail in such a wind.

He depended upon the brisk sea breeze and the strong ebb tide, which together kicked up a nasty sea, to bring me to grief. But I was on my mettle, and never in all my life did I sail a boat better than on that day. I was keyed up to concert pitch, my brain was working smoothly and quickly, my hands never fumbled once, and it seemed that I almost divined the thousand little things which a small-boat sailor must be taking into consideration every second.

It was Demetrios who came to grief instead. Something went wrong with his centre-board, so that it jammed in the case and would not go all the way down.   In a moment's breathing space, which he had gained from me by a clever trick, I saw him working impatiently with the centre-board, trying to force it down. I gave him little time, and he was compelled quickly to return to the tiller and sheet.

The centre-board made him anxious.   He gave over playing with me, and started on the long beat to Vallejo.   To my joy, on the first long tack across, I found that I could eat into the wind just a little bit closer than he. Here was where another man in the boat would have been of value to him; for, with me but a few feet astern, he did not dare let go the tiller and run amidships to try to force down the centre-board.

Unable to hang on as close in the eye of

the wind as formerly, he proceeded to slack his sheet a trifle and to ease off a bit, in order to outfoot me. This I permitted him to do till I had worked to windward, when I bore down upon him. As I drew close, he feinted at coming about. This led me to shoot into the wind to forestall him. But it was only a feint, cleverly executed, and he held back to his course while I hurried to make up lost ground.

He was undeniably smarter than I when it came to manœuvring. Time after time I all but had him, and each time he tricked me and escaped. Besides, the wind was freshening constantly, and each of us had his hands full to avoid capsizing. As for my boat, it could not have been kept afloat but for the extra ballast. I sat cocked over the weather gunwale, tiller in one hand and sheet in the other; and the sheet, with a single turn around a pin, I was very often forced to let go in the severer puffs. This allowed the sail to spill the wind, which was equivalent to taking off so much driving power, and of course I lost ground. My consolation was that Demetrios was as often compelled to do the same thing.

The strong ebb-tide, racing down the Straits in the teeth of the wind, caused an unusually heavy and spiteful sea, which dashed aboard continually. I was dripping wet, and even the sail was wet half-way up the after leech. Once I did succeed in outmanœuvring Demetrios, so that my bow bumped into him amidships. Here was where I should have had another man. Before I could run forward and leap aboard, he shoved the boats apart with an oar, laughing mockingly in my face as he did so.

We were now at the mouth of the Straits,

in a bad stretch of water. Here the Vallejo Straits and the Carquinez Straits rushed directly at each other. Through the first flowed all the water of Napa River and the great tide-lands; through the second flowed all the water of Suisun Bay and the Sacramento and San Joaquin rivers. And where such immense bodies of water, flowing swiftly, clashed together, a terrible tide-rip was produced. To make it worse, the wind howled up San Pablo Bay for fifteen miles and drove in a tremendous sea upon the tide-rip.

Conflicting currents tore about in all directions, colliding, forming whirlpools, sucks, and boils, and shooting up spitefully into hollow waves which fell aboard as often from leeward as from windward. And through it all, confused, driven into a madness of motion, thundered the great smoking seas from San Pablo Bay.

I was as wildly excited as the water. The boat was behaving splendidly, leaping and lurching through the welter like a race-horse. I could hardly contain myself with the joy of it. The huge sail, the howling wind, the driving seas, the plunging boat — I, a pygmy, a mere speck in the midst of it, was mastering the elemental strife, flying through it and over it, triumphant and victorious.

And just then, as I roared along like a conquering hero, the boat received a frightful smash and came instantly to a dead stop. I was flung forward and into the bottom. As I sprang up I caught a fleeting glimpse of a greenish, barnacle-covered object, and knew it at once for what it was, that terror of navigation, a sunken pile. No man may guard against such a thing. Water-logged and floating just beneath the surface, it was impossible to sight it in the troubled water in time to escape.

The whole bow of the boat must have been crushed in, for in a few seconds the boat was half full. Then a couple of seas filled it, and it sank straight down, dragged to bottom by the heavy ballast. So quickly did it all happen that I was entangled in the sail and drawn under. When I fought my way to the surface, suffocating, my lungs almost bursting, I could see nothing of the oars. They must have been swept away by the chaotic currents. I saw Demetrios Contos looking back from his boat, and heard the vindictive and mocking tones of his voice as he shouted exultantly. He held steadily on his course, leaving me to perish.

There was nothing to do but to swim for it, which, in that wild confusion, was at the best a matter of but a few moments. Holding my breath and working with my hands, I managed to get off my heavy sea-boots and my jacket. Yet there was very little breath I could catch to hold, and I swiftly discovered that it was not so much a matter of swimming as of breathing.

I was beaten and buffeted, smashed under by the great San Pablo whitecaps, and strangled by the hollow tide-rip waves which flung themselves into my eyes, nose, and mouth. Then the strange sucks would grip my legs and drag me under, to spout me up in some fierce boiling, where, even as I tried to catch my breath, a great whitecap would crash down upon my head.

It was impossible to survive any length of time. I was breathing more water than air, and drowning all the time. My senses began to leave me, my head to whirl around. I struggled on, spasmodically, instinctively, and was barely half conscious when I felt myself caught by the shoulders and hauled over the gunwale of a boat.

For some time I lay across a seat where I had been flung, face downward, and with the water running out of my mouth. After a while, still weak and faint, I turned around to see who was my rescuer. And there, in the stern, sheet in one hand and tiller in the other, grinning and nodding good-naturedly, sat Demetrios Contos. He had intended to leave me to drown, — he said so afterward, — but his better self had fought the battle, conquered, and sent him back to me.

"You all-a right?" he asked.

I managed to shape a "yes" on my lips, though I could not yet speak.

"You sail-a de boat verr-a good-a," he said. "So good-a as a man."

A compliment from Demetrios Contos was a compliment indeed, and I keenly appreciated it, though I could only nod my head in acknowledgment.

We held no more conversation, for I was busy recovering and he was busy with the boat. He ran in to the wharf at Vallejo, made the boat fast, and helped me out. Then it was, as we both stood on the wharf, that Charley stepped out from behind a net-rack and put his hand on Demetrios Contos's arm.

"He saved my life, Charley," I protested; "and I don't think he ought to be arrested."

A puzzled expression came into Charley's face, which cleared immediately after, in a way it had when he made up his mind.

"I can't help it, lad," he said kindly. "I can't go back on my duty, and it's plain duty to arrest him. To-day is Sunday; there are two salmon in his boat which he caught to-day. What else can I do?"

"But he saved my life," I persisted, unable to make any other argument.

"There, in the stern, sat Demetrios Contos."

Demetrios Contos's face went black with rage when he learned Charley's judgment. He had a sense of being unfairly treated. The better part of his nature had triumphed, he had performed a generous act and saved a helpless enemy, and in return the enemy was taking him to jail.

Charley and I were out of sorts with each other when we went back to Benicia. I stood for the spirit of the law and not the letter; but by the letter Charley made his stand. As far as he could see, there was nothing else for him to do. The law said distinctly that no salmon should be caught on Sunday. He was a patrolman, and it was his duty to enforce that law. That was all there was to it. He had done his duty, and his conscience was clear. Nevertheless, the whole thing seemed unjust to me, and I felt very sorry for Demetrios Contos.

Two days later we went down to Vallejo to the trial.   I had to go along as a witness, and it was the most hateful task that I ever performed in my life when I testified on the witness stand to seeing Demetrios catch the two salmon Charley had captured him with.

Demetrios had engaged a lawyer, but his case was hopeless.   The jury was out only fifteen minutes, and returned a verdict of guilty. The judge sentenced Demetrios to pay a fine of one hundred dollars or go to jail for fifty days.

Charley stepped up to the clerk of the court. "I want to pay that fine," he said, at the same time placing five twenty-dollar gold pieces on the desk.   "It — it was the only way out of it, lad," he stammered, turning to me.

The moisture rushed into my eyes as I seized his hand.   "I want to pay —" I began.

"To pay your half?" he interrupted.   "I certainly shall expect you to pay it."

In the meantime Demetrios had been informed by his lawyer that his fee likewise had been paid by Charley.

Demetrios came over to shake Charley's hand, and all his warm Southern blood flamed in his face. Then, not to be outdone in generosity, he insisted on paying his fine and lawyer's fee himself, and flew half-way into a passion because Charley refused to let him.

More than anything else we ever did, I think, this action of Charley's impressed upon the fishermen the deeper significance of the law. Also Charley was raised high in their esteem, while I came in for a little share of praise as a boy who knew how to sail a boat. Demetrios Contos not only never broke the law again, but he became a very good friend of ours, and on more than one occasion he ran up to Benicia to have a gossip with us.

VII

YELLOW HANDKERCHIEF

YELLOW HANDKERCHIEF

"I'M not wanting to dictate to you, lad," Charley said; "but I'm very much against your making a last raid. You've gone safely through rough times with rough men, and it would be a shame to have something happen to you at the very end."

"But how can I get out of making a last raid?" I demanded, with the cocksureness of youth. "There always has to be a last, you know, to anything."

Charley crossed his legs, leaned back, and considered the problem. "Very true. But why not call the capture of Demetrios Contos the last? You're back from it safe and sound and hearty, for all your good wetting, and — and —" His voice broke and he could not speak for a moment. "And I could never forgive myself if anything happened to you now."

I laughed at Charley's fears while I gave in to the claims of his affection, and agreed to consider the last raid already performed. We had been together for two years, and now I was leaving the fish patrol in order to go back and finish my education. I had earned and saved money to put me through three years at the high school, and though the beginning of the term was several months away, I intended doing a lot of studying for the entrance examinations.

My belongings were packed snugly in a sea-chest, and I was all ready to buy my ticket and ride down on the train to Oakland, when Neil Partington arrived in Benicia. The *Reindeer* was needed immediately for work far down on the Lower Bay, and

Neil said he intended to run straight for Oakland. As that was his home and as I was to live with his family while going to school, he saw no reason, he said, why I should not put my chest aboard and come along.

So the chest went aboard, and in the middle of the afternoon we hoisted the *Reindeer's* big mainsail and cast off. It was tantalizing fall weather. The sea-breeze, which had blown steadily all summer, was gone, and in its place were capricious winds and murky skies which made the time of arriving anywhere extremely problematical. We started on the first of the ebb, and as we slipped down the Carquinez Straits, I looked my last for some time upon Benicia and the bight at Turner's Shipyard, where we had besieged the *Lancashire Queen*, and had captured Big Alec, the King of the Greeks. And at the mouth of the Straits I looked with not a little interest upon the spot where a few days before I should have drowned but for the good that was in the nature of Demetrios Contos.

A great wall of fog advanced across San Pablo Bay to meet us, and in a few minutes the *Reindeer* was running blindly through the damp obscurity. Charley, who was steering, seemed to have an instinct for that kind of work. How he did it, he himself confessed that he did not know; but he had a way of calculating winds, currents, distance, time, drift, and sailing speed that was truly marvellous.

"It looks as though it were lifting," Neil Partington said, a couple of hours after we had entered the fog. "Where do you say we are, Charley?"

Charley looked at his watch. "Six o'clock, and three hours more of ebb," he remarked casually.

"But where do you say we are?" Neil insisted.

Charley pondered a moment, and then answered, "The tide has edged us over a bit out of our course, but if the fog lifts right now, as it is going to lift, you'll find we're not more than a thousand miles off McNear's Landing."

"You might be a little more definite by a few miles, anyway," Neil grumbled, showing by his tone that he disagreed.

"All right, then," Charley said, conclusively, "not less than a quarter of a mile, not more than a half."

The wind freshened with a couple of little puffs, and the fog thinned perceptibly.

"McNear's is right off there," Charley said, pointing directly into the fog on our weather beam.

The three of us were peering intently in

that direction, when the *Reindeer* struck with a dull crash and came to a standstill. We ran forward, and found her bowsprit entangled in the tanned rigging of a short, chunky mast. She had collided, head on, with a Chinese junk lying at anchor.

At the moment we arrived forward, five Chinese, like so many bees, came swarming out of the little 'tween-decks cabin, the sleep still in their eyes.

Leading them came a big, muscular man, conspicuous for his pock-marked face and the yellow silk handkerchief swathed about his head. It was Yellow Handkerchief, the Chinaman whom we had arrested for illegal shrimp-fishing the year before, and who, at that time, had nearly sunk the *Reindeer*, as he had nearly sunk it now by violating the rules of navigation.

"What d'ye mean, you yellow-faced hea-

then, lying here in a fairway without a horn
a-going?" Charley cried hotly.

"Mean?" Neil calmly answered. "Just
take a look — that's what he means."

Our eyes followed the direction indicated
by Neil's finger, and we saw the open amidships of the junk, half filled, as we found
on closer examination, with fresh-caught
shrimps. Mingled with the shrimps were
myriads of small fish, from a quarter of an
inch upward in size. Yellow Handkerchief
had lifted the trap-net at high-water slack,
and, taking advantage of the concealment
offered by the fog, had boldly been lying by,
waiting to lift the net again at low-water slack.

"Well," Neil hummed and hawed, "in
all my varied and extensive experience as a
fish patrolman, I must say this is the easiest
capture I ever made. What'll we do with
them, Charley?"

"Tow the junk into San Rafael, of course," came the answer. Charley turned to me. "You stand by the junk, lad, and I'll pass you a towing line. If the wind doesn't fail us, we'll make the creek before the tide gets too low, sleep at San Rafael, and arrive in Oakland to-morrow by midday."

So saying, Charley and Neil returned to the *Reindeer* and got under way, the junk towing astern. I went aft and took charge of the prize, steering by means of an antiquated tiller and a rudder with large, diamond-shaped holes, through which the water rushed back and forth.

By now the last of the fog had vanished, and Charley's estimate of our position was confirmed by the sight of McNear's Landing a short half-mile away. Following along the west shore, we rounded Point Pedro in plain view of the Chinese shrimp villages, and a

" I went aft and took charge of the prize."

great to-do was raised when they saw one of their junks towing behind the familiar fish patrol sloop.

The wind, coming off the land, was rather puffy and uncertain, and it would have been more to our advantage had it been stronger. San Rafael Creek, up which we had to go to reach the town and turn over our prisoners to the authorities, ran through wide-stretching marshes, and was difficult to navigate on a falling tide, while at low tide it was impossible to navigate at all. So, with the tide already half-ebbed, it was necessary for us to make time. This the heavy junk prevented, lumbering along behind and holding the *Reindeer* back by just so much dead weight.

"Tell those coolies to get up that sail," Charley finally called to me. "We don't want to hang up on the mud flats for the rest of the night."

I repeated the order to Yellow Handkerchief, who mumbled it huskily to his men. He was suffering from a bad cold, which doubled him up in convulsive coughing spells and made his eyes heavy and bloodshot. This made him more evil-looking than ever, and when he glared viciously at me I remembered with a shiver the close shave I had had with him at the time of his previous arrest.

His crew sullenly tailed on to the halyards, and the strange, outlandish sail, lateen in rig and dyed a warm brown, rose in the air. We were sailing on the wind, and when Yellow Handkerchief flattened down the sheet the junk forged ahead and the tow-line went slack. Fast as the *Reindeer* could sail, the junk outsailed her; and to avoid running her down I hauled a little closer on the wind. But the junk likewise outpointed, and in a couple of minutes I was abreast of the *Rein-*

deer and to windward. The tow-line had now tautened, at right angles to the two boats, and the predicament was laughable.

"Cast off!" I shouted.

Charley hesitated.

"It's all right," I added. "Nothing can happen. We'll make the creek on this tack, and you'll be right behind me all the way up to San Rafael."

At this Charley cast off, and Yellow Handkerchief sent one of his men forward to haul in the line. In the gathering darkness I could just make out the mouth of San Rafael Creek, and by the time we entered it I could barely see its banks. The *Reindeer* was fully five minutes astern, and we continued to leave her astern as we beat up the narrow, winding channel. With Charley behind us, it seemed I had little to fear from my five prisoners; but the darkness prevented my keeping a sharp eye on them, so I transferred my revolver from my trousers pocket to the side pocket of my coat, where I could more quickly put my hand on it.

Yellow Handkerchief was the one I feared, and that he knew it and made use of it, subsequent events will show.   He was sitting a few feet away from me, on what then happened to be the weather side of the junk. I could scarcely see the outlines of his form, but I soon became convinced that he was slowly, very slowly, edging closer to me.   I watched him carefully.   Steering with my left hand, I slipped my right into my pocket and got hold of the revolver.

I saw him shift along for a couple of inches, and I was just about to order him back — the words were trembling on the tip of my tongue — when I was struck with great force by a heavy figure that had leaped through the air upon me from the lee side. It was one of the crew. He pinioned my right arm so that I could not withdraw my hand from my pocket, and at the same time clapped his other hand over my mouth. Of course, I could have struggled away from him and freed my hand or gotten my mouth clear so that I might cry an alarm, but in a trice Yellow Handkerchief was on top of me.

I struggled around to no purpose in the bottom of the junk, while my legs and arms were tied and my mouth securely bound in what I afterward found to be a cotton shirt. Then I was left lying in the bottom. Yellow Handkerchief took the tiller, issuing his orders in whispers; and from our position at the time, and from the alteration of the sail, which I could dimly make out above me as a blot against the stars, I knew the junk was being headed into the mouth of a small slough which emptied at that point into San Rafael Creek.

In a couple of minutes we ran softly alongside the bank, and the sail was silently lowered. The Chinese kept very quiet. Yellow Handkerchief sat down in the bottom alongside of me, and I could feel him straining to repress his raspy, hacking cough. Possibly seven or eight minutes later I heard Charley's voice as the *Reindeer* went past the mouth of the slough.

"I can't tell you how relieved I am," I could plainly hear him saying to Neil, "that the lad has finished with the fish patrol without accident."

Here Neil said something which I could not catch, and then Charley's voice went on:

"The youngster takes naturally to the water, and if, when he finishes high school, he takes a course in navigation and goes deep sea, I see no reason why he shouldn't rise to be master of the finest and biggest ship afloat."

It was all very flattering to me, but lying there, bound and gagged by my own prisoners, with the voices growing faint and fainter as the *Reindeer* slipped on through the darkness toward San Rafael, I must say I was not in quite the proper situation to enjoy my smiling future. With the *Reindeer* went my last hope. What was to happen next I could not imagine, for the Chinese were a different race from mine, and from what I knew I was confident that fair play was no part of their make-up.

After waiting a few minutes longer, the crew hoisted the lateen sail, and Yellow Handkerchief steered down toward the mouth of San Rafael Creek. The tide was getting lower, and he had difficulty in escaping the mud-banks. I was hoping he would run aground, but he succeeded in making the Bay without accident.

As we passed out of the creek a noisy discussion arose, which I knew related to me. Yellow Handkerchief was vehement, but the other four as vehemently opposed him. It was very evident that he advocated doing away with me and that they were afraid of the consequences. I was familiar enough with the Chinese character to know that fear alone restrained them. But what plan they offered in place of Yellow Handkerchief's murderous one, I could not make out.

My feelings, as my fate hung in the balance, may be guessed. The discussion developed into a quarrel, in the midst of which Yellow Handkerchief unshipped the heavy tiller and sprang toward me. But his four companions threw themselves between, and a clumsy struggle took place for possession of the tiller.

In the end Yellow Handkerchief was overcome, and sullenly returned to the steering, while they soundly berated him for his rashness.

Not long after, the sail was run down and the junk slowly urged forward by means of the sweeps. I felt it ground gently on the soft mud. Three of the Chinese — they all wore long sea-boots — got over the side, and the other two passed me across the rail. With Yellow Handkerchief at my legs and his two companions at my shoulders, they began to flounder along through the mud. After some time their feet struck firmer footing, and I knew they were carrying me up some beach. The location of this beach was not doubtful in my mind. It could be none other than one of the Marin Islands, a group of rocky islets which lay off the Marin County shore.

When they reached the firm sand that marked high tide, I was dropped, and none too gently. Yellow Handkerchief kicked me spitefully in the ribs, and then the trio floundered back through the mud to the junk. A moment later I heard the sail go up and slat in the wind as they drew in the sheet. Then silence fell, and I was left to my own devices for getting free.

I remembered having seen tricksters writhe and squirm out of ropes with which they were bound, but though I writhed and squirmed like a good fellow, the knots remained as hard as ever, and there was no appreciable slack. In the course of my squirming, however, I rolled over upon a heap of clam-shells — the remains, evidently, of some yachting party's clam-bake. This gave me an idea. My hands were tied behind my back; and, clutching a shell in them, I rolled over and over, up the beach, till I came to the rocks I knew to be there.

Rolling around and searching, I finally discovered a narrow crevice, into which I shoved the shell. The edge of it was sharp, and across the sharp edge I proceeded to saw the rope that bound my wrists. The edge of the shell was also brittle, and I broke it by bearing too heavily upon it. Then I rolled back to the heap and returned with as many shells as I could carry in both hands. I broke many shells, cut my hands a number of times, and got cramps in my legs from my strained position and my exertions.

While I was suffering from the cramps, and resting, I heard a familiar halloo drift across the water. It was Charley, searching for me. The gag in my mouth prevented me from replying, and I could only lie there, helplessly fuming, while he rowed past the island and his voice slowly lost itself in the distance.

I returned to the sawing process, and at the end of half an hour succeeded in severing the rope. The rest was easy. My hands once free, it was a matter of minutes to loosen my legs and to take the gag out of my mouth. I ran around the island to make sure it *was* an island and not by any chance a portion of the mainland. An island it certainly was, one of the Marin group, fringed with a sandy beach and surrounded by a sea of mud. Nothing remained but to wait till daylight and to keep warm; for it was a cold, raw night for California, with just enough wind to pierce the skin and cause one to shiver.

To keep up the circulation, I ran around the island a dozen times or so, and clambered across its rocky backbone as many times more — all of which was of greater service to me,

as I afterward discovered, than merely to
warm me up. In the midst of this exercise
I wondered if I had lost anything out of my
pockets while rolling over and over in the
sand. A search showed the absence of my
revolver and pocket-knife. The first Yellow Handkerchief had taken; but the knife
had been lost in the sand.

I was hunting for it when the sound of
rowlocks came to my ears. At first, of course,
I thought of Charley; but on second thought
I knew Charley would be calling out as he
rowed along. A sudden premonition of
danger seized me. The Marin Islands are
lonely places; chance visitors in the dead
of night are hardly to be expected. What
if it were Yellow Handkerchief? The sound
made by the rowlocks grew more distinct.
I crouched in the sand and listened intently.
The boat, which I judged a small skiff from

the quick stroke of the oars, was landing in
the mud about fifty yards up the beach. I
heard a raspy, hacking cough, and my heart
stood still. It was Yellow Handkerchief.
Not to be robbed of his revenge by his more
cautious companions, he had stolen away
from the village and come back alone.

I did some swift thinking. I was unarmed
and helpless on a tiny islet, and a yellow bar-
barian, whom I had reason to fear, was
coming after me. Any place was safer than
the island, and I turned instinctively to the
water, or rather to the mud. As he began
to flounder ashore through the mud, I started
to flounder out into it, going over the same
course which the Chinese had taken in landing me and in returning to the junk.

Yellow Handkerchief, believing me to be
lying tightly bound, exercised no care, but
came ashore noisily. This helped me, for,

under, the shield of his noise and making no more myself than necessary, I managed to cover fifty feet by the time he had made the beach. Here I lay down in the mud. It was cold and clammy, and made me shiver, but I did not care to stand up and run the risk of being discovered by his sharp eyes.

He walked down the beach straight to where he had left me lying, and I had a fleeting feeling of regret at not being able to see his surprise when he did not find me. But it was a very fleeting regret, for my teeth were chattering with the cold.

What his movements were after that I had largely to deduce from the facts of the situation, for I could scarcely see him in the dim starlight. But I was sure that the first thing he did was to make the circuit of the beach to learn if landings had been made by other boats. This he would have known at once by the tracks through the mud.

Convinced that no boat had removed me from the island, he next started to find out what had become of me. Beginning at the pile of clam-shells, he lighted matches to trace my tracks in the sand. At such times I could see his villanous face plainly, and, when the sulphur from the matches irritated his lungs, between the raspy cough that followed and the clammy mud in which I was lying, I confess I shivered harder than ever.

The multiplicity of my footprints puzzled him. Then the idea that I might be out in the mud must have struck him, for he waded out a few yards in my direction, and, stooping, with his eyes searched the dim surface long and carefully. He could not have been more than fifteen feet from me, and had he lighted a match he would surely have discovered me.

He returned to the beach and clambered about over the rocky backbone, again hunting for me with lighted matches. The closeness of the shave impelled me to further flight. Not daring to wade upright, on account of the noise made by floundering and by the suck of the mud, I remained lying down in the mud and propelled myself over its surface by means of my hands. Still keeping the trail made by the Chinese in going from and to the junk, I held on until I reached the water. Into this I waded to a depth of three feet, and then I turned off to the side on a line parallel with the beach.

The thought came to me of going toward Yellow Handkerchief's skiff and escaping in it, but at that very moment he returned to the beach, and, as though fearing the very thing I had in mind, he slushed out through the mud to assure himself that the skiff was safe.

This turned me in the opposite direction. Half swimming, half wading, with my head just out of water and avoiding splashing, I succeeded in putting about a hundred feet between myself and the spot where the Chinese had begun to wade ashore from the junk. I drew myself out on the mud and remained lying flat.

Again Yellow Handkerchief returned to the beach and made a search of the island, and again he returned to the heap of clam-shells. I knew what was running in his mind as well as he did himself. No one could leave or land without making tracks in the mud. The only tracks to be seen were those leading from his skiff and from where the junk had been. I was not on the island. I must have left it by one or the other of those two tracks. He had just been over the one to his skiff, and was certain I had not left that way. Therefore I could have left the island only by going over the tracks of the junk landing. This he proceeded to verify by wading out over them himself, lighting matches as he came along.

When he arrived at the point where I had first lain, I knew, by the matches he burned and the time he took, that he had discovered the marks left by my body. These he followed straight to the water and into it, but in three feet of water he could no longer see them. On the other hand, as the tide was still falling, he could easily make out the impression made by the junk's bow, and could have likewise made out the impression of any other boat if it had landed at that particular spot. But there was no such mark; and I knew that he was absolutely convinced that I was hiding somewhere in the mud.

But to hunt on a dark night for a boy in a

sea of mud would be like hunting for a needle in a haystack, and he did not attempt it. Instead he went back to the beach and prowled around for some time. I was hoping he would give me up and go, for by this time I was suffering severely from the cold. At last he waded out to his skiff and rowed away. What if this departure of Yellow Handkerchief's were a sham? What if he had done it merely to entice me ashore?

The more I thought of it the more certain I became that he had made a little too much noise with his oars as he rowed away. So I remained, lying in the mud and shivering. I shivered till the muscles of the small of my back ached and pained me as badly as the cold, and I had need of all my self-control to force myself to remain in my miserable situation.

It was well that I did, however, for, possibly an hour later, I thought I could make out something moving on the beach. I watched intently, but my ears were rewarded first, by a raspy cough I knew only too well. Yellow Handkerchief had sneaked back, landed on the other side of the island, and crept around to surprise me if I had returned.

After that, though hours passed without sign of him, I was afraid to return to the island at all. On the other hand, I was almost equally afraid that I should die of the exposure I was undergoing. I had never dreamed one could suffer so. I grew so cold and numb, finally, that I ceased to shiver. But my muscles and bones began to ache in a way that was agony. The tide had long since begun to rise, and, foot by foot, it drove me in toward the beach. High water came at three o'clock, and at three o'clock I drew myself up on the beach, more dead than alive, and too helpless to have offered any resistance had Yellow Handkerchief swooped down upon me.

But no Yellow Handkerchief appeared. He had given me up and gone back to Point Pedro. Nevertheless, I was in a deplorable, not to say a dangerous, condition. I could not stand upon my feet, much less walk. My clammy, muddy garments clung to me like sheets of ice. I thought I should never get them off. So numb and lifeless were my fingers, and so weak was I, that it seemed to take an hour to get off my shoes. I had not the strength to break the porpoise-hide laces, and the knots defied me. I repeatedly beat my hands upon the rocks to get some sort of life into them. Sometimes I felt sure I was going to die.

But in the end, — after several centuries, it seemed to me, — I got off the last of my clothes. The water was now close at hand, and I crawled painfully into it and washed the mud from my naked body. Still, I could not get on my feet and walk and I was afraid to lie still. Nothing remained but to crawl weakly, like a snail, and at the cost of constant pain, up and down the sand. I kept this up as long as possible, but as the east paled with the coming of dawn I began to succumb. The sky grew rosy-red, and the golden rim of the sun, showing above the horizon, found me lying helpless and motion-less among the clam-shells.

As in a dream, I saw the familiar mainsail of the *Reindeer* as she slipped out of San Rafael Creek on a light puff of morning air. This dream was very much broken. There are intervals I can never recollect on looking back over it. Three things, however, I distinctly remember: the first sight of the *Rein-*

deer's mainsail; her lying at anchor a few hundred feet away and a small boat leaving her side; and the cabin stove roaring red-hot, myself swathed all over with blankets, except on the chest and shoulders, which Charley was pounding and mauling unmercifully, and my mouth and throat burning with the coffee which Neil Partington was pouring down a trifle too hot.

But burn or no burn, I tell you it felt good. By the time we arrived in Oakland I was as limber and strong as ever, — though Charley and Neil Partington were afraid I was going to have pneumonia, and Mrs. Partington, for my first six months of school, kept an anxious eye upon me to discover the first symptoms of consumption.

Time flies. It seems but yesterday that I was a lad of sixteen on the fish patrol. Yet I know that I arrived this very morning from China, with a quick passage to my credit, and master of the barkentine *Harvester*. And I know that to-morrow morning I shall run over to Oakland to see Neil Partington and his wife and family, and later on up to Benicia to see Charley Le Grant and talk over old times. No; I shall not go to Benicia, now that I think about it. I expect to be a highly interested party to a wedding, shortly to take place. Her name is Alice Partington, and, since Charley has promised to be best man, he will have to come down to Oakland instead.